THE BURNING
QUESTIONS
OF BINGO BROWN

Also available in Large Print
by Betsy Byars:

Cracker Jackson
The 18th Emergency
The Not Just Anybody Family

THE BURNING
QUESTIONS
OF BINGO BROWN

BETSY BYARS

G.K.HALL&CO.
Boston, Massachusetts
1989

Copyright © Betsy Byars, 1988.

Published in Large Print by arrangement with
Viking Penguin Inc.

G.K. Hall Large Print Book Series.

Set in 18 pt. Plantin.

Library of Congress Cataloging in Publication Data

Byars, Betsy Cromer.
  The burning questions of Bingo Brown.

  (G.K. Hall large print book series)
  Summary: A boy is puzzled by the comic and confusing questions
of youth and worried by disturbing insights into adult conflicts.
  1. Large type books. [1. Large type books]
I. Title.
[PZ7.B9836Bu   1989]   [Fic]   88-35791
ISBN 0-8161-4770-1 (lg. print)

CONTENTS

THE BURNING
QUESTIONS
OF BINGO BROWN

DR. JEKYLL AND MS. HYDE

BINGO BROWN fell in love three times during English class.

Bingo had never been in love before. He had never even worried about falling in love. He thought love couldn't start until a person had zits, so he had plenty of time. Bingo was worried about being called on.

It was the kind of assignment Bingo dreaded. "You are successes," Mr. Markham had told them. "You are tops in your field. Your picture has been on the cover of *Time*. I have written to you for advice because I want to be exactly like you. Now write a letter back to me. Describe your career and give me some advice."

1

Bingo's letter was face-down on his desk. His arms were crossed over it.

Tara Emerson was reading her letter. Tara had picked a career that she said was physically hard but rewarding and brought pleasure to millions of people. Tara was a Solid Gold dancer.

"Could I be a Solid Gold dancer?" Mr. Markham asked when she was through. He was twirling a yellow Scripto pencil between his thin fingers. He was better at twirling than a majorette.

"I don't think so," Tara said.

"Why not? Are they all girls?"

"No, but the boys are hunks," Tara said.

There was an amused murmur. Mr. Markham stopped twirling his pencil and looked around the room, his bright, unsmiling eyes as sharp as a bird of prey's.

When Mr. Markham looked like that, as if he were going to pounce, Bingo wondered why he had wanted to be in Mr. Markham's class, why he had run all the way home to yell, "Mom! I got Mr. Mark!"

Mr. Markham said, "Melissa, I'd like to hear your letter."

Melissa said, "I've got two careers, Mr. Markham. Is that all right?"

"It's your life."

Melissa stood up. "I'm a scientist and a rock star," she said.

Her words electrified Bingo. He stopped breathing. It was exactly like a movie he had seen recently called *Dr. Jekyll and Mr. Hyde.*

He had a stunning picture of Melissa in the starring role. She was in a laboratory pouring formulas from one vial to another. Then as night approached, she threw off her white lab coat, spraypainted her hair different colors, and jumped into a limousine.

The picture of Melissa at a rock concert, on stage in a wild pink spotlight, was even more stunning: Bingo couldn't help himself. He fell instantly in love with Dr. Jekyll and Ms. Hyde.

Although Bingo had had no previous

experience with love, he knew that this was not a fleeting, everyday kind of love. This was a love that would go on till the end of time. A love for eternity. Maybe even infinity.

Harriet Conway got up next. Harriet was a conductor. Bingo started breathing again. He knew he could never lose his heart to a train conductor. Even if he was not already in love, he—

Then he heard the rest. Harriet was the conductor of a symphony orchestra! When Bingo heard that, he was electrified all over again.

This time he saw Harriet on stage. She was dressed in the outfit that the good witch wore in *The Wizard of Oz*. She even had the tiara. The wand was her baton.

Bingo saw himself in the front row of the concert hall. His hair was combed down as flat and shiny as a Ken doll's.

This concerto, Harriet said, pointing the baton at him, *is dedicated to Bingo, without whose help tonight would not have been possible. Bingo, will you stand?*

Not only would he stand, but he would turn and bow to the right and left and—

Bingo broke off. He was actually on his feet. He was bowing!

"Not yet, Bingo," Mr. Markham said mildly. "I'll tell you when. Gang, I know how eager you all are to read your letters, but I must ask you to wait until you are called on. Can you wait just a little longer, Bingo?"

"I'll try."

Bingo sat down. His face burned. He was now in love with two girls. Five minutes ago he had been carefree, totally unattached romantically, and now he loved two girls and loved them both for eternity, maybe even infinity. He hoped the *National Enquirer* didn't get wind of it. BOY LOVES TWO GIRLS FOR INFINTY, SETS WORLD RECORD.

Mr. Markham said, "Mamie Lou."

Mamie Lou got up. Mamie Lou was the biggest girl in the room, and since Bingo was the smallest boy, she had never appealed to him. Also Billy

Wentworth had told Bingo that Mamie Lou wore brassieres. The last thing on Bingo's mind was falling in love with a girl who wore brassieres.

Mamie Lou began to read. Mamie Lou, it turned out, was President of the United States.

Bingo stiffened. It was like being hit by lightning three times in a row. As Mamie Lou's husband, he would be First Gentleman of the United States of America.

Visions mushroomed in his mind—Airforce One . . . Camp David . . . Russia. He would accompany Mamie Lou everywhere. At summit meetings he would not go shopping with the other presidents' wives. He would sit at Mamie Lou's side. They would have a ranch and he would take up horseback riding. He would be a popular First Gentleman and fill in for Mamie Lou at parades and Easter-egg rolls. Barbara Walters would—

"Bingo?"

"What?"

"Now, Bingo, now," Mr. Markham said. "This is the moment you've been waiting for."

"What moment?"

"Your letter, Bingo. You have one, don't you?"

"Oh, yes, sure, but it's not very good."

"It will not be, I assure you, the first thing I have heard in this classroom that was 'not very good'. What advice do you have for me?"

Bingo got up. He cleared his throat.

"Dear Mr. Markham,
As the leading science-fiction writer in the world today, I am glad that you asked me for advice. The best advice I can give you is to buy all of my books. Then read them. I am enclosing the opening paragraphs from a few of my best-sellers so that you can see what you have to shoot for."

Bingo paused. "Mr. Mark, you want me to read the paragraphs?"

"I am, as they say, all ears."

Bingo cleared his throat again.

"At eight-thirty the earth beneath the city began to move. The tremor measured nine on the Richter scale. People thought it was an earthquake. The animals knew better. The animals knew that what had moved beneath the city was alive, alive after four thousand years of sleep! It was alive and it was coming up!"

Bingo paused. "You want the next one?"

"Please."

"It's sort of short."

"Read."

"Something was stirring deep within the volcano on the island of Mau Mau, and it was not lava." He looked up at Mr. Markham. "You want the next one? It's kind of like the others, only it takes place in the Arctic."

"Bingo, don't make me beg. I want them all. Every last one. All!"

"This is all. It's the last one." Bingo turned the paper around so Mr. Markham could see for himself.

Mr. Markham closed his eyes as if he were tired. "Bingo, read."

"Yes, sir.

"Deep within the frozen Arctic, the ice that had been untouched for one thousand years was beginning to melt. Something hot stirred in the tundra."

Mr. Markham opened his eyes. "That's it, Bingo?"

"That's it."

"Well, I'm not sure anyone can top the magnificent spell Bingo has woven, but who would like to give it a try?"

As Bingo sat down, he made a decision. If Mr. Markham called on another girl, he was going to put his

9

fingers in his ears. He could not fall in love a fourth time. He understood now his weakness for powerful women.

Bingo got his fingers ready to put in his ears.

Billy Wentworth turned around. Out of the side of his mouth he said, "You were wrong, Worm Brain."

"About what?"

"Your paper wasn't 'not very good.' "

"Oh, thanks."

"It was rotten."

Billy Wentworth had been drawing a python on his arm with a Magic Marker. He flexed his muscle, and the python writhed toward Bingo.

Mr. Markham said, "Billy, I'd like to hear your letter."

Mr. Markham always called on Billy when he talked out of the side of his mouth, but Billy had not yet caught on to this.

Billy stood. He smoothed down his Rambo t-shirt. He said, "I'll tell mine, Mr. Mark, if you don't mind. Everybody knows I'm going to be a member of the Special Services division of the armed forces."

"I didn't know it."

"Come on, Mr. Mark. Don't—"

"You didn't write a letter?"

"Oh, I wrote one." Billy tapped the side of his head. "It's up here. I can say it if you want me to. It'll be like an oral composition."

"Did I ask for oral compositions? Is this a lesson in recitation?" Mr. Markham slumped forward, the Scripto pencil pressing into his chest. His eyes looked as hurt as if the pencil had pierced his heart.

"The only way you can restore my faith in you, Billy, is to hand in the letter about your career in the armed services tomorrow. Can you manage that, Billy? Otherwise I'll have to write a letter of my own—to your mommy."

"Sure, Mr. Mark, no problem."

The bell rang then, but Bingo kept sitting at his desk. He was so burdened by the three unwanted loves that he was not sure he could walk. Dr. Jekyll and Ms. Hyde. The orchestra conductor. The president of the United States of America. Loving important women like that was tiring.

Bingo wondered if anybody else had ever been in love with three such women. Or could this be just the beginning? His heart sank. Was he going to fall in love with three girls every day? How long could he keep it up? How many girls were there in Roosevelt Middle School? How could he find out? Would the office tell him? He had to know, because the total number of girls, divided by three, would be the length of time it would take him to fall in love with all of them. It made an impressive formula.

After that, what? Would he have to transfer to another school? Another city? Would he spend his youth desperately searching for three new girls, then three more new girls, then—

"Bingo."

"What?"

"The—bell—rang," Mr. Markham

12

said. He was strapping on his motorcycle helmet. He spoke as carefully as he would have spoken to an infant. "School—is—over. You—may—go—home—now."

"Oh, thanks."

"You—are—welcome."

Bingo got up quickly and left the room.

MOUSSE ATTACK

IT WAS midnight. Bingo was in the bathroom, staring at himself in the mirror.

The face looking back at him was tired, but the eyes were restless, too bright. I look like Mr. Markham, Bingo thought.

He turned his face from side to side, checking out the similarity. Yes, it's the eyes, he thought.

Could it be possible that Mr. Markham was also in love with three women? Could that account for the way he looked lately?

Should I say something? Bingo wondered. Something like, "I know how you feel, Mr. Markham, because we're in the same fix." Should he hold up three fingers? Or should—

"What are you doing in the bathroom, Bingo?" his mother called.

Bingo opened the medicine cabinet and fumbled noisily.

"I'm trying to find the junior aspirin," he called back.

"What's wrong? Are you sick?"

"No. Don't bother getting up, Mom. I'm not sick."

"Then why do you need aspirin?"

"I can't sleep. Oh, here they are. I found them. Don't get up."

Bingo did not want to face his mom. She might make him tell her the reason he could not sleep. His mother would definitely not be sympathetic about his being in love with three girls.

"You can't do anything without going totally overboard, can you?" she would say.

14

"Well," she called from her bedroom, "take the aspirin and go back to bed."

"That's what I'm trying to do."

The aspirin didn't help much, and Bingo spent a restless night chasing Dr. Jekyll and Ms. Hyde, the Orchestra Conductor, and the President of the United States, none of whom wanted to be caught. The final chase scene took place on the White House lawn and was broadcast on the CBS evening news.

In the morning Bingo was even more haggard. He stumbled into the breakfast room, sat down, and knocked over his milk. "Sorry," he said. "I just caught a glimpse of myself in the toaster."

His mom said, "Honestly, Bingo, you get more like your father every day."

His dad said, "Say thank you, Bingo. Your mom just paid you a great compliment."

"Thank you, Mom."

His mother did not look amused. She started pulling napkins out of the holder and laying them over the milk. She said, "You get exactly two things from your father—his clumsiness at the table and his freckles." She sat down.

Bingo's mom hated freckles. The first thing she had asked in the delivery room after Bingo was born was, "Is he freckled?"

"Not yet," the doctor answered.

This was not the first thing said in the delivery room, however, when Bingo was born. The first thing the doctor said was, "Bingo!" He probably said this every time a baby popped out, but Bingo's mother thought it was a first. "Mom, he wasn't naming me," Bingo had said once. This was when he was in kindergarten and they were learning a song about a dog named Bingo. The song went like this:

B-I-N-G-O
B-I-N-G-O
And Bingo was his name—O!

Everytime they sang that, tears of

shame would come to Bingo's eyes. He felt as bad as if he'd been named Fido or Poochie.

Anyway, Bingo's father was very freckled. He told Bingo one time that he had counted his freckles and he had five thousand, two hundred and twenty-four of them.

Bingo was impressed. "How do you know that?"

"Well, I took a ruler," his father said, "and I marked off one square inch on the back of my hand, right there. I counted all the freckles in that square inch—there were seventeen and a half."

"There can't be a half of a freckle. There can be a small freckle but—"

"It was on the line—half in, half out."

"Oh."

"Then I found out how many square inches of skin there are on the human body, and I multiplied by seventeen and a half, and it came out five thousand, two hundred and twenty-four."

Bingo stood up. "May I please be excused?" he asked.

"You haven't eaten a thing."

"Mom, I can't help it. I've got something on my mind—three somethings."

"Oh, all right, you may be excused."

Bingo got up and headed for the bathroom. Perhaps a Yogi Bear vitamin would . . .

Bingo opened the medicine cabinet and reached for the vitamins. His hand stopped in midair.

There was a new product in the medicine cabinet. He took out the can and read a new word. *Mousse.*

The instructions were simple. *Spray an egg-size ball of mousse into the palm of your hand.*

Bingo did that. His egg was the size of a dinosaur egg, and he felt better.

Apply to hair and style as usual.

Bingo's usual method of styling was to comb. He applied the mousse, combed, and looked in the mirror.

For a moment Bingo could not move. He had transformed himself. Here, in

18

the mirror, was not the haggard, pained face of last night. Here was the boy he had always wanted to be. When he got to school, every girl in her right mind would fall in love with him. He was going to have to hire a bodyguard like Sly Stallone or become a recluse like Michael Jackson.

"Why are you standing there smiling at yourself?" his mom asked from the doorway.

"I like the way I look with this mousse on my hair."

"There's such a thing as too much mousse."

"Mom, some people need a lot of mousse."

"You overdo everything."

The last thing a boy in love with three girls wanted to hear was a lecture on overdoing things. "I'm off to school," he said cheerfully, glancing at himself one last time.

As he went out the door, he wondered if mousse could bring new happiness to Mr. Mark. What would be the best way to let Mr. Markham know about mousse? Should he write an anonymous note? Should he wait until the class went out to recess and write the word on the blackboard in capital letters? Mousse! Would the class know he had written it? Would it give away the secret of his new looks? He wanted Mr. Markham to have the secret because they shared a similar pain, but he didn't want Billy Wentworth to know.

As he went down the steps, he asked one last question. If Billy Wentworth does find out, will he start calling me Mousse Head?

INSULTS AND BURNING QUESTIONS

BINGO SPENT the morning inspecting the girls he was in love with. This was because he hoped to discover something he had previously overlooked—a wart, a mustache, a loose tooth, anything that would turn him off. If he could fall out of love with just one of them, that would be a major breakthrough.

Would it be conspicuous, he wondered, if he brought his dad's binoculars? If he could look at them through the zoom lens, wouldn't he be sure to—

"Bingo!"

"Oh, sorry, Mr. Mark. Did you want something?"

"Class, from now on, assume that if I call your name, I want something. Like, I just called Bingo's name—what does that mean? All together!"

"You want something!"

"What do you want?" Bingo asked.

"I want you to pass out the notebooks."

"I'd be glad to." With the confidence of a newly moussed person, he got up, accepted the notebooks, and made his way down the rows.

Mr. Markham said, "Gang, these are going to be your journals. They are your property. They will stay in your desks. Part of every day will be spent writing in your journals."

After he had given out the notebooks, Bingo sat down quickly and opened his journal. He felt he should be the first one to start writing. After all, he had announced the day before that he was the top science-fiction writer in the world.

He looked up. Others had beat him to it. Mamie Lou . . . even Billy Wentworth. What did they have to be writing about?

Bingo decided to check this out. Weeks before, he had worked out his route to the pencil sharpener.

As he passed Billy's desk, he glanced down.

Billy Wentworth was not writing after all. He was drawing a picture of himself in combat gear and labeling the various weapons—flamethrower, radio-control missile, noxious-gas grenades, etc.

Bingo kept walking. He wanted to see what his three loves were writing in their journals. Hopefully it would be something to weaken his love.

The first one he came to was Mamie Lou. She was not writing at the moment, but she had written two words previously. Now she was lost in thought. Bingo glanced down. He read the two words.

Dear Dairy,

Bingo blinked his eyes twice, three times. Was Mamie Lou, the President of the United States, writing to a bunch of cows? He reread the words.

Dear Dairy,

"Excuse me for interrupting, but I think you've made a mistake." Bingo said this in the respectful way he would have corrected any President of the United States. "You've written *Dear Dairy,* and you probably meant to write *Dear Diary.* See, the *i* goes where the *a* is, and the *a*—"

23

Mamie Lou looked up at him and Bingo trailed off.

This was not a look of gratitude. This was a look of pure, ice-cold hatred. It was the look that would probably be effective, years from now, against Russian diplomats, but to look at him that way, he who was going to fill in for her at Easter-egg rolls . . .

Billy Wentworth exploded into laughter. "Dear Dairy," he said, "Mooooooo-oooooooo." More Wentworth laughter. Billy's laughs were distinctive *Har, har, har*'s.

Mr. Markham closed his eyes as if in pain. He had told them last week that when he closed his eyes in this manner, he did not want to hear one single sound.

"This is important, gang, so let's practice," he had said. "Make as much noise as you want to."

The class had made a moderate amount of noise.

"Is that the best you can do? You disappoint me."

24

They had made a lot of noise with whistles and catcalls. Mr. Markham had closed his eyes. There was silence.

"One more time."

More noise. Eyes closed. Silence.

"I think you've got it. I hope so."

Bingo waited, frozen in place, until Mr. Markham opened his eyes. When Mr. Markham's newly opened eyes looked right at Bingo, Bingo decided to go back to his seat without sharpening his pencil or checking any more journals.

Bingo was disappointed. All he had learned was that the President of the United States did not take criticism well and that he would have to use a lot of tact to help her through her presidency.

Bingo raised his hand. "You're not going to read these, right?"

"No one is worried about *me* reading them, Bingo. Who are you worried about, class? Who will be going to the pencil sharpener again and again and reading over your shoulders? Who? All together now—but not too loud."

"Bingo."

The hushed sound of his name broke Bingo's writer's block. He knew now what he would write. This journal was going to be one of the most important books of the century. It was going to be a book of questions, burning questions . . .

He folded his book open and wrote on the title page:

BURNING QUESTIONS
by
Bingo Brown

On the next page, he began to write questions, starting with a couple that had been worrying him a lot.

Has there ever been a successful writer named Bingo?

Has there ever been a successful writer with freckles?

Has there ever been a successful person with freckles?

Why did no one notice my mousse?

Does mousse wear off?

26

Should I bring a bottle of mousse in my lunch box instead of a thermos?

What does Mr. Markham think about when he closes his eyes?

When the bell for recess rang, Bingo did not hurry out with the rest of the class. He still had questions to put in his journal and, also, he did not have the strength—because of the burdens of love—to go out to recess.

"Mr. Mark, is it all right if I stay in?"

"No."

"I'll keep my head on my desk."

"No."

"Why not?"

"Because I want to put my head on my desk, and I know I'll keep lifting my head to make sure *your* head is on *your* desk and that way *my* head will never be on *my* desk. Does that make any sense to you, Bingo?"

"Yes, sir."

"Thank you and good-bye."

When Bingo got to the playground, he saw that Billy Wentworth had pulled out a book of insults and was reading things like, "Helen McTeer is so ugly she isn't listed in *Who's Who*, she's listed in *What's That*." Billy Wentworth was going around the playground, finding an insult for every single person there.

Mamie Lou's insult was, "Mamie Lou, you are a perfect 10. Your face is a two, your body is a two, your legs are a two—" Mamie Lou didn't wait around to hear what her other two's were.

Tom Knott's was, "Tom, your nose is so big that it has its own zip code."

Melissa's was, "Melissa, you have the face of a saint—a Saint Bernard."

The Orchestra Conductor's was, "Harriet, you may not have invented ugliness, but you sure are the local distributor."

Miss Fanucci, the music teacher, chose that moment to come out onto the playground to round up some chorus members, and Billy found an insult for her.

Hers was, "Miss Fanucci is so ugly that when she goes to the zoo she has to buy two tickets—one to get in and one to get out."

Miss Fanucci passed the group at the exact moment Billy delivered the line. She stopped. She put out her hand for the book. She was not smiling.

Billy whipped the book behind his back. The faint remnants of the Magic Marker python writhed on his bare arm.

Miss Fanucci kept holding out her hand.

Billy Wentworth shook his head regretfully.

Miss Fanucci said, "Billy."

Billy said, "The book isn't mine, Miss Fanucci, it belongs to my dad. He's got to have it."

Miss Fanucci's hand was still extended. The class pulled back like old-time Westerners sensing a shoot-out. For the first time in the school year they were absolutely quiet.

"Miss Fanucci," Billy said, "I might

as well level with you. My dad's going to a roast for one of his bowling buddies on Friday night, and he's got to have this book. If he doesn't, he won't have any insults. You wouldn't want my dad to go to a roast without any insults, would you? He would be disgraced."

Miss Fanucci hesitated.

"Do you want my dad to never bowl again, Miss Fanucci? Because if my dad got disgraced in front of his buddies, then that's what would happen. I know the man, Miss Fanucci. I've been living with him for thirteen years."

Miss Fanucci then did what anybody in their right mind would have done. She lowered her hand. "I don't want to see that book again, Billy."

Billy dropped it down the neck of his Rambo t-shirt and patted it. "You won't," he said.

Before he went back inside, Billy managed to remember the insult he had picked out for Bingo.

"Bingo is so freckled that flies never

land on him. They can't find the right spot. Har, har, har."

THE END OF AN IMPERFECT DAY

Bingo was quiet at supper that night. It had been a long tiring day, but his brain was still actively turning out questions for his journal.

Like: *Did the look Mamie Lou gave me mean that she does not want me to be First Gentleman? Do I really want to be First Gentleman if she's going to look at me like that?*

And: *What did Harriet and Melissa write in their journals? How can I find out, now that Mr. Mark has alerted the class to the reason for my trips to the pencil sharpener?*

And: *Is there more wrong with Mr. Markham than mousse can fix?*

Bingo was so occupied that he barely heard the excited chatter of his parents. He kept sitting there, sifting through the questions, discarding some, keeping others, and at the same time he was making shish kebab on his fork—one lima bean, one piece of macaroni, one square of ham. Bingo liked to mix his flavors.

His mother was saying, "I've hated living next door to an empty house. It gives me the creeps to see dark windows. I will just be so, soooo glad to have neighbors again, won't you?"

His father said, "Yes."

She turned to Bingo. "And more good news. The people who have bought the house have a son your age. They moved to town last summer but had to sell their house back in Beauford before they could buy."

Bingo speared another piece of macaroni, completing the shish kebab.

"In fact, he's in your room at school."

Bingo put the food in his mouth.

"Their name is Wentworth."

As soon as the name *Wentworth* was spoken, the two lima beans, two pieces of macaroni, two squares of ham all went directly into Bingo's windpipe.

The next few minutes were spent with both his parents competing to give him the Heimlich maneuver.

"Let me!"

"No, me!"

His mom won. The lima beans and the macaroni and one ham square popped out.

"Are you all right?" his dad asked.

He couldn't answer, just kept shaking his head. Tears rolled down his cheeks.

"Of course he's not all right," his mom said. "Look at him."

She gave him one more sharp jab under the ribs, and the ham popped out. Satisfied at last, she said, "If you'd take time to chew your food, Bingo, things like this wouldn't happen."

They sat back down. Finally Bingo managed to choke out the words, "Did you say *Wentworth?*"

"Yes, he's with National Cash Register and she's a nurse. There's a boy—I believe his name is Billy—and a girl two years older."

The pieces of food felt like they had fossilized in his windpipe, permanent memories of the worst moment of his life.

"Can I be excused?"

"Bingo, you haven't eaten a thing."

"I can't . . . my throat."

"Well, drink your milk."

He took four swallows. "Is that enough?"

"Yes, I guess so, but after this, Bingo, only put into your mouth what you can chew and swallow. Don't cram your mouth with food. You overdo everything."

"I know."

As he left the room, his mom went back to her happy recital of the new neighbors. Bingo staggered to his room and fell across the bed.

Now he knew the true meaning of burning questions, because his brain was being seared with them.

Does Billy Wentworth know I live in this house?

How long can I keep him from finding out?

What then?

"Bingo, what are you doing? It's almost one o'clock in the morning."

Bingo was in the bathroom, going through the medicine cabinet. "Mom, we're out of junior aspirin!"

"Go back to bed, Bingo."

"And mousse!"

"I hope you're not putting mousse on your head at one o'clock in the morning."

"No, I was looking for an aspirin because I can't sleep and when I picked up the mousse can to look behind it, I noticed how light the can was. Mom, it's empty!"

His mom got out of bed and came down the hall. "Don't wake up your dad, Bingo, he has a trip tomorrow."

"Look, Mom, it's empty."

"You must have used it all up."

"I used three measly dinosaur eggs of mousse, one before school, one before supper, one before bedtime. I needed three eggs of mousse. Don't you remember how my hair used to look?"

"Your hair looked fine."

"You told the barber one time that my hair was 'riddled with cowlicks.' I had to ask what the word *riddled* meant."

"I said no such thing. Anyway, you're only supposed to use mousse after you shampoo."

"Who says?"

"The label."

"Where?"

"Right there."

"Anyway, I did shampoo."

"When? Last week? Last month?"

They would probably have continued the argument because Bingo's mom was a good arguer, and she had passed on this trait to Bingo, but Bingo's dad called out, "Will you two shut up? I'll buy more mousse. I'll buy a truckload of mousse. I'll buy a warehouse of the stuff if you'll just shut up."

"Good night, Bingo," his mother said.

"Good night, Mom."

TO RAY FROM WORM BRAIN

IT WAS English again, and Bingo sat staring at his sheet of paper. This was one of the assignments he had been looking forward to. This was the day they were writing to their favorite authors.

Bingo had already decided he would write to Ray Bradbury and reveal to him that he had three science-fiction novels underway. Even though he still had only one paragraph done on each one, he figured Ray Bradbury did not get many letters from twelve-year-olds who have started three novels.

However, the fact that Billy Wentworth was going to move next door to him occupied his whole mind. So far, Billy didn't know. Bingo could tell that from the way he said, "Hello, Worm Brain," in his usual way, but when Billy Wentworth did find out, he was not going to like it.

The class had now been working on their letters for fifteen minutes. All Bingo had on his paper were two words.

Dear Ray,

Bingo sighed. He decided to do what he usually did in blank moments—sharpen his pencil and check out the other letters. He'd be very surprised if he saw any other Dear Ray's.

He got up. He knew he would have to walk very briskly so it wouldn't look suspicious. He passed one Lloyd Alexander, one Jean Fritz and one Dr. Seuss. This took him to the desk of the President of the United States.

He glanced down. He was so astonished by her letter that all thoughts of Billy Wentworth went out of his mind.

The President of the United States was writing to Laura Ingalls Wilder.

And not only that, she had written this unbelievable sentence:

Dear Laura Ingalls Wilder,
  I know that you are dead, but please write if you can and let me know where you get your ideas.

And this was the woman that he thought he loved! This was the woman he was going to sit beside at conferences and fill in for at Easter-egg rolls!

She looked up at him then, giving him the same icy-cold look she had given him the day before. "What are you looking at?" she asked.

"Nothing."

"Then bug off."

Bingo continued on his way to the pencil sharpener. He felt a deep sense of relief. Now he definitely only loved two girls, and perhaps if he saw who they were writing to, he wouldn't love them either.

Dr. Jekyll and Ms. Hyde saw him

coming, unfortunately, and turned her paper over so Bingo couldn't see it.

Bingo stood there stabbing himself on the leg with his pencil.

Why do people care if I see their papers? Do they think my eyes will ruin the words? Why can't they let me look? Why? Why? Why?

Mr. Markham stopped Bingo's questions with one of his own. "What are you doing, Bingo?"

"Nothing. Going to the pencil sharpener."

"Have you finished your letter?"

"Not quite."

"Anyway, Bingo, I do not want the letters written in pencil. Intelligent beings do not write letters in pencil. They write in pen. This is because they are secure enough not to need to erase."

"I'm doing my first draft in pencil."

Bingo sharpened his pencil and spun around so fast he caught Dr. Jekyll and Ms. Hyde off-guard. She was writing to Isaac Asimov!

This moved Bingo so much that he

40

couldn't step away from her desk. He could not move. He just stood there, staring down at her hair which was so beautiful she didn't even need mousse. He was glued in place, rooted to the spot. He would never ever leave her desk. He would spend the rest of his life here like a pilgrim, a worshipper at a shrine, a—

"Bingo, either go directly to your desk or the principal's office."

"Yes, sir."

Bingo found that these harsh words from Mr. Markham broke the spell, releasing him, and he was now capable of returning to his desk.

Bingo was the only person at the supper table who was depressed. His parents were extremely happy. They were acting like children and Bingo was acting like an elderly person.

Here's what transformed Bingo's parents. They got letters from their college—they went to the same college, that's how they met—and their college was going to have something special for the homecoming game. They were inviting back all the former cheerleaders to lead a cheer in unison at halftime, and all the former bandmembers to play the fight song, hopefully also in unison.

Bingo's mom had played the trumpet in the college band and his dad had been head cheerleader, and a lot of their friends were cheerleaders and band members and would be coming too.

Halfway through the meal Bingo's dad got up to look for his cheerleader sweater. His mom didn't look for *her* uniform. Band members didn't get to keep their uniforms, of course; they had to turn them in. She still had her trumpet, though, and after supper she was going to practice.

Bingo finally managed to break in with, "Mom, have you heard any more about the Wentworths?"

"The who?"

Bingo's mom was already mentally

on the football field blasting out the fight song. She looked blank because she thought the Wentworths were somebody she knew in college. "Oh, you mean next door," she said.

"Yes, I meant next door."

"They're moving in next Friday."

This time fortunately Bingo did not have any food in his mouth so all that went down his windpipe was spit. Still, if you inhale enough spit, you can get just about as choked on it as on shish kebabs.

Finally he stopped coughing long enough to ask, "What's their hurry?"

"Their hurry? That's a funny question. Well, I imagine they would like to get settled as soon as possible. I've met her and she's very nice. The son was there, and I asked him if he knew you and he said he did."

Bingo's heart missed a beat. "Mom! You asked Billy Wentworth if he knew me?"

"Yes, what's wrong with that?"

"Mom!"

"It was a perfectly natural question."

"What exactly did you say?"

"I said, 'I believe my son's in your room. His name's Bingo. Do you know him?' And he said, 'Yes.' "

"How did he say it, Mom, did he say it in a normal voice or did he—"

Bingo didn't get to finish because his dad appeared in the doorway. His dad had found his cheerleading sweater and put it on. It was tight, and there was a moth-hole over his heart, but those imperfections didn't bother him at all. He came into the kitchen doing a cheer.

ONE—TWO—THREE—FOUR
THREE—TWO—ONE—FOUR
WHO FOR?
WHAT FOR?
WHO YOU GONNA YELL FOR?
CATAWBA! CATAWBA!
CATAWBA!

Bingo tried not to appear as horrified as he was. He could not look at his mom because he felt so sorry for her being married to his dad.

To his surprise, his mom clapped her hands together. She jumped up. Her napkin flew into the air. "I'll get my trumpet," she yelled.

She reappeared with her trumpet and began playing the college fight song, and his father—what had gotten into the man?—began doing a sort of Highland fling.

All Bingo could do to help them was to pray that no one would come to the door. If anyone saw his family at this moment, the family name of Brown would go down, as they say, in infamy.

A burning question to put in his notebook tomorrow:

What, exactly, is infamy?

THE T-SHIRT WAR

Bingo managed to be late for school the next day so that Billy Wentworth wouldn't be able to say anything to

him. Oh, he would be able to say something out of the side of his mouth,
something like, "I don't like living next
door to Worm Brains," nothing could
prevent that, but Bingo wouldn't have
to answer.

As Bingo came through the door, Mr.
Markham said, "Get in your seat,
Bingo. I have an announcement from
our distinguished principal and, as
usual, it will deeply affect us all. I don't
want anyone claiming they didn't hear
it."

Bingo sat.

These announcements didn't usually
affect him, so he began fumbling under
his desk for his journal. He wanted to
jot down a few quick questions.

Then he heard the announcement,
and his journal fell to the floor along
with the fragile structure of his life.

" 'In the future,' " Mr. Markham
read, " 'no one will be allowed to wear
t-shirts that have any writing on
them.' "

There was such a long and terrible

46

silence that Mr. Markham read the announcement again.

" 'In the future, no one will be allowed to wear t-shirts that have any writing on them.' "

Bingo had spent half the night planning to have a t-shirt printed up which read:

I AM A NONVIOLENT PERSON.
PLEASE RESPECT MY COMMITMENT
BY NOT HITTING ME.

Now his commitment to nonviolence could never be worn to school. He could wear it in his yard, of course; in fact he didn't plan to go out in the yard in anything else. Still, it was a bitter disappointment.

Now a ripple of anger replaced the silence. Bingo joined in the murmurings. Every single person in the room, it turned out, was as affected as he was.

The President of the United States raised her hand.

"Yes, Mamie Lou."

Mamie Lou had on her Beach Boys t-shirt.

"That's not fair."

"Maybe not, Mamie Lou, but there have been complaints from some of the parents. A few of the older boys have been wearing shirts that were vulgar, and since we don't have time to check every word on every shirt, from now on there will be no t-shirts with writing. Gang, this affects me as much as it does you. I can't wear my Beethoven Or Bust anymore."

Billy Wentworth put up his hand.

"Yes, Billy?"

"What did the vulgar shirts say?"

Mr. Markham closed his eyes. When he opened them he said, "Now, gang, come on. Take out your arithmetic books, please. Once again we are going to have a stab at dividing fractions. I'm hoping for some sort of a breakthrough."

Billy's hand was in the air again.

"Billy, if this question is about the vulgarity on the t-shirts . . ."

"It's not."

Mr. Markham twirled his pencil and waited.

Billy stood up. He smoothed the front of his Rambo t-shirt. Although Bingo could only see the back of Billy's head, he knew that at that moment Rambo and Billy wore the same tough expression.

Billy pointed to the word *Rambo*. "Would this count as writing?"

"Let's see, Billy. Are those what you would call your ABC's?"

Billy did not answer. He put his hands behind his back in a military stance.

"All right, gang, here's a good rule to follow. If your shirt has any of the ABC's on it—and I hope you know them by now—if it has any of the ABC's on it, you can't wear it to school."

Billy kept standing there.

"What now, Billy?"

"I want a ruling on this shirt."

"Billy—"

"An official ruling."

Mr. Markham sighed.

"Because I'm wearing it no matter what."

Billy sat down to applause.

Bingo spent the rest of math drawing pictures in his journal. These were pictures of the t-shirts which he would no longer be able to wear to school: MOZART FREAK, I LOVE THE SMITHSONIAN, his GENERIC t-shirt, BODY UNDER CONSTRUCTION . . .

He then drew a picture of Melissa as he would never (because of the principal's cruel and unjust ruling) get to see her—in a t-shirt that said DR. JEKYLL AND MS. HYDE.

He was giving Melissa some extra curls when Billy Wentworth turned around. This happened so fast Bingo didn't have time to shield his picture.

Billy Wentworth said, "I'm moving next door to you."

Bingo said, "I know."

Bingo was proud that his voice sounded almost normal.

After lunch the official ruling from the principal's office came down on Billy's Rambo t-shirt. Mr. Markham read it aloud.

" 'Any writing, any word of any kind will not be permitted. If Billy's Rambo t-shirt has a word on it, it falls into that category. Billy's Rambo t-shirt will no longer be permitted at this school.' "

Mr. Markham put the paper on his desk. "It is as I feared. If even *one* of the dreaded ABC's is on the shirt, it can't be worn, gang."

Billy slammed his history book shut and threw it under his desk.

As the sound of the book against metal echoed through the classroom, it sounded like the opening shot of a long and bloody war.

Bingo made a quick decision. He would have several of the nonviolent shirts made. Billy Wentworth's anger might spill over onto an innocent victim. The innocent victim might be him.

He would stop at The T-Shirt Factory on the way home.

"Come on," Mr. Markham said tiredly. "Give me a break."

THE BOY BEHIND
THE REBEL LEADER

BINGO'S DAD left the supper table to answer a phone call. "You bet I'll be there," Bingo heard him say. "I wouldn't miss homecoming for anything."

While Bingo and his mom continued to eat, they had a surprising conversation. Bingo started it.

"Oh, guess what, Mom?" he said.

"What?"

"From now on, no one in our school is allowed to wear t-shirts that have any words whatsoever on them."

"Oh?"

Bingo began to list the individual injustices so that she could see the enormity of their losses.

"Billy Wentworth—he's the boy that's moving next door—can't wear his Rambo. Mamie Lou can't wear Beach Boys, Melissa can't wear her very beautiful, baby-blue Care Bears shirt, Amy Myers can't wear her Mickey Mouse shirt because—get this, Mom—it has the words *Walt Disney Productions* under Mickey's face."

"Why did they decide this?"

"Somebody, not me, but somebody wore a vulgar shirt. We think we know who it was, and because this one boy wore this one shirt, and it did have something vulgar on it—I won't tell you what unless you force me because it was very, very vulgar."

"I won't force you."

"Anyway, the words were all run together with no spaces in between and so none of the teachers noticed it, but some girl—and we think we know who she is too—went home and told her mother."

"Fink," his mom said.

"Mom!"

"Well, she shouldn't have told."

"Actually she didn't tell. She was too ashamed to tell. She wrote it on a sheet of paper just the way it had been on the shirt."

"She's still a fink."

"Mom!"

"Go on."

"So her mom looked at the words and finally she got them separated and she was furious. She called the principal and threatened to call the Board of Education."

"But that's terrible—to punish the entire school for the actions of one boy."

"I know."

"Grossly unfair."

"I think so too."

"You students ought to protest."

"What?"

"You students should rebel and *you* ought to lead the rebellion!"

"Me? Me lead them?"

"Yes, you could do it. I'm sure you could. Why don't you set the protest for, say, Friday. You could call it in a wear-in."

"A what?"

"A wear-in. You know, like a sit-in, only this will be a wear-in. Everyone in the school must—" She held up one finger for emphasis. "—must wear a t-shirt that says something. And you, as the leader, must wear one that says *Principals Stink.*"

"Mom!"

Now Bingo was really shocked. He couldn't believe his mom was advocating this. Usually she didn't like for him to stick out in a crowd, much less lead one.

"I will be extremely disappointed in anything less," she finished firmly.

"Mom, are you serious?"

Bingo didn't get the answer because his father came back from his phone call. "You'll never guess who that was."

"Fig Newton," his mom said. "Fig always makes you laugh like that."

"He and his wife—second wife—are coming and—"

"May I be excused?" Bingo said.

"Yes, go on, go on," his mom said. She seemed eager for him to get on with the revolutionary plans. "Who's the second wife? I thought . . ."

Bingo went to his room with a heavy heart. Despite his mother's encouragement, he could not lead the rebellion. Like all moms, she was blind to his inabilities.

He looked at himself in the mirror, searching for some characteristic of rebel leadership that he had previously overlooked. If only he had a little mustache.

His shoulders slumped.

He was not now and never could be a rebel leader. It was hopeless. He sank onto the bed. In the morning he would break the news to his mom. "I'm just not a Billy Wentworth," he would say.

Billy Wentworth. Bingo got up slowly. He looked at himself again in the mirror.

No, he could not be the leader, but he could be the boy behind the leader. He *did* have the characteristic for that—knowing a leader to get behind. Maybe he could fulfill his mother's dreams after all.

He started for the living room. His mom was practicing "Fight, Darn You, Fight" on the trumpet. His dad was pulling on his cheerleading sweater. Bingo decided not to interrupt. There would be time to tell them of his triumph later.

During the long night, as Bingo tossed and turned in his Superman pajamas, he tried out different strategies. "Billy, would you mind leading a rebellion for my mom?" Or, "Billy, I was thinking of having a rebellion and I was wondering if you would like to lead it." Or, "Billy, do you like danger and intrigue?"

Finally he tried the truth. "Billy, my mom had an interesting suggestion about our t-shirt problem."

Bingo got out of bed at once and

stood in front of the mirror. "Billy, my mom had an interesting suggestion about our t-shirt problem." Not bad for an opener . . .

An hour later, wrapped in his Superman cape, he fell asleep murmuring for the forty-fourth time, "Billy, my mom had an interesting suggestion about . . ."

THE RISE OF
THE REBEL LEADER

THE CLASSROOM was quiet the next morning. Billy Wentworth had on his Rambo t-shirt, but he had put a strip of black tape over the word *Rambo*. Bingo thought this had the effect of making it look worse than it was, like the black strips they put on nudes to hide vital stuff.

The girls wore unfamiliar blouses and dresses, and the boys, ill-fitting shirts. Bingo had on a t-shirt with one-fortieth of the American flag on it. This was from camp last summer. On parents' night, forty campers had stood together on a hill, creating the American flag, and had sung a medley of patriotic songs.

Bingo took a deep breath and touched Billy's shoulder. When Billy turned around he said, "Mymomhadaninterestingsuggestionabout—"

Billy said, "What?"

Bingo started over. "My mom had—"

Mr. Markham said, "Quiet, gang, no talking. This means you too, Bingo."

Bingo said, "I'll tell you later, Billy."

Mr. Markham got up from his desk. He was twirling his yellow Scripto pencil in a new way, weaving it through his fingers so fast Bingo couldn't keep up with it.

"I have an important assignment for you," he said. He looked up at the ceiling, apparently working out the details in his mind. Then he looked down, somehow looking directly at every single one of them. Only Mr. Markham could do that.

"I want you to write a letter for me, and, gang, this will be the most important letter you have ever written in your life."

Billy mumbled, "Here we go again, gang."

Bingo felt uneasy. He didn't like the way Mr. Markham looked. Mr. Markham put his pencil behind his ear and took hold of his chin as if he had an imaginary beard. He stroked the invisible beard. His eyes were too bright.

He said, "Has any one in this classroom ever seen my girlfriend?"

There was a shocked silence. Most of them had never thought of Mr. Markham as a romantic person who went on dates and had girlfriends. The boys looked down at their desks in embarrassment.

Even Bingo, who had previously thought he and Mr. Markham might share an unfortunate fate—being in love with three women—even Bingo didn't want to hear about one *particular* girl-friend.

"Nobody has seen her?"

Melissa put her hand halfway up.

"You've seen her, Melissa?"

"I don't know. Maybe." Melissa glanced around as if she were looking for help. "One time I saw somebody on the back of your motorcycle."

"Could you be a little more specific, Melissa? After all, a great many girls have ridden on the back of my bike."

"Her name was Dawn."

"That's the one. Tell the class, Melissa, did you get a good look at her?"

"Pretty good." Melissa was twisting her hair now. Bingo had never seen her so uneasy. "You got off and went in the grocery store and she stayed on the motorcycle. I went over and said, 'Hi.' "

"Melissa, would you say Dawn is beautiful, very beautiful, or incredibly beautiful?"

"She was real pretty."

"I'll take that. Now, Melissa, for those who have not seen her, would you stand up and describe her?"

Melissa sighed.

"Please, Melissa."

"I'm not good at describing people."

"Try."

Melissa got up slowly. "Well, she's about that tall." Melissa held her hand three inches over her head. "She's got long blonde hair and it's real curly. I don't know what color her eyes are because she had on dark glasses."

"Green."

"She reminded me of Malibu Barbie. Can I please sit down now?"

"Yes. The point is, gang, that Dawn is very beautiful, but she is not incredibly smart. I guess you can't have it all. So every now and then Dawn comes up with something stupid like—like she might say she wants to break up with me. She does *not* want to break up," he went on quickly. "I want to make that clear. What she wants is to be talked out of breaking up with me. You understand what I'm saying?"

He looked at them, again with eyes that were too bright, to see if they understood. Apparently satisfied, he went on.

"That is what we are going through right now. Dawn says she wants to break up with me, and I need a new way to convince her not to. I need a new approach, gang, and that's where you come in. I thought if you would write her letters, telling her how great I am, telling her why she shouldn't break up with me—you know the kind of letters I want, don't you?"

He leaned forward and watched them. This time he must have seen doubt in their faces. "All right, how many will write a letter?"

No hands went up.

"Come on, this is an assignment. You are refusing an assignment? Melissa, you'll write, won't you?"

Melissa didn't look at him. "I wouldn't know what to say."

"Just tell the truth. That's all I'm asking. *Dear Dawn, I do not want you to break up with Mr. Markham because he is the most wonderful teacher in the world.* Something like that. Be funny if you want to. *Dear Dawn, Do not break up with Mr. Mark because as soon as he is free, women will be breaking down the door of our classroom, and we won't be able to have math.* Be sad. Make her cry. *Dear Dawn, Mr. Markham only has two months to live.* They're your letters."

Bingo's mouth was hanging open, and his was not the only one.

"All right," Mr. Markham went on in a firmer voice, "I have given you an assignment and I want you to get out your paper. Write *Dear Dawn,* and something will come to you. I guarantee it. Come on, gang. I need these letters."

Over the rustle of paper, Mr. Markham said, "Normally, I don't place any limits on length, but I do think the descriptions of my good qual-

64

ities should be kept to no more than three pages." He laughed, but nobody else did.

"Get started, gang. I'd like to have these by recess."

Bingo bent over his paper instantly and began to write. He was aware that he was the only person in the class who had started. His pencil flew across the lined paper.

Billy, he wrote, *my mom had an interesting suggestion about our t-shirt problem.*

"Bingo!" Mr. Markham cried in a pleased way. "I knew I could count on you!"

Bingo shrugged and kept writing.

She said we ought to rebel. She said we ought to set aside one day—like this Friday—and every single person in the school would wear a shirt with words on it. She said it would be a wear-in. Like a sit-in. She said . . .

Later, after he gave the letter to Billy, he had time to scribble:

Dear Dawn,
Please, please don't break up with
Mr. Markham.

> Hurriedly, but most sincerely,
> Bingo Brown

The playground buzzed with questions.

"What did you say to Dawn?"

"I didn't know what to say. What did you say?"

"I didn't want to hand mine in, did you?"

"You think Mr. Mark's flipped his lid?"

And then came the big question: "Hey, what's Wentworth doing on top of the garbage can?"

Bingo had the answer to that one. "I think he's going to make an announcement. It looks like that's what he's going to do. Come on. Let's see what he's going to say. It may be about the t-shirts."

Bingo closed in around the garbage can with the others. His heart had moved up into his throat. This was his work. He had done this. He wished his mom could have been there to share his pride.

"I got an announcement," Wentworth said. "Let me put that another way. I got a command."

He had their attention now. Not one person moved. All eyes were riveted on the figure in the Rambo t-shirt. Billy Wentworth's face was so stern, so hard, he made Rambo look like a wimp.

"On Friday," he said, "everybody in this school is going to wear a t-shirt with something written on it. Did you girls in the back hear that?"

The girls nodded.

"I'm going to say it one more time, and that's it. I'm not asking you. I am telling you. On Friday—that's this Friday—everybody in this school is going to wear a t-shirt with something written on it."

There was another silence. Bingo put his hand on his throat to keep his heart from going up any higher.

"If there is anybody here that has not got the guts to do that, then now is the time to step out and say, 'I ain't got the guts. I'm not going to do it.'"

The only movement was heads turning around to see if anyone had the guts to step out and say they didn't have the guts. There was not one gutless person on the playground.

"Any questions?"

There were no questions.

"Pass it on," Billy Wentworth said. Then he got down from the garbage can.

The garbage can was made of tough, industrial-strength steel, but the top had been permanently indented by the weight of Billy's combat boots. He walked away, and everyone looked with awe at the garbage lid. It was as if they were in front of Grauman's Chinese Theater, looking at the footprints of a star.

The bell rang, and Bingo hurried in to write down his burning questions of the afternoon.

Has a principal ever expelled an entire school?

Will I have time to get a t-shirt that says PRINCIPALS STINK?

Will Mr. Markham notice that my letter to Dawn is short? Should I get it back and add a P.S? What could the P.S. be?

Is my life ever going to be calm?

TWO SETBACKS IN THE T-SHIRT WAR

BINGO RAN all the way home from school. At last he had something to tell his mom that would make her proud of him. He burst into the kitchen.

"It worked!"

His mom was on the phone, selling Mary Kay cosmetics. His mom wanted a job in marketing, but was filling in the gap with Mary Kay cosmetics. She held up her hand for silence.

Bingo sat down at the table and waited eagerly for her to finish. When she hung up, he said again, "Mom, it worked!"

"What worked?"

Bingo could see that she was not interested in his news, but, oh boy, was she going to be! "Your suggestion!"

"What suggestion." Still no interest.

"The wear-in!"

Now she looked up. She said, again, "What?" This time she dragged the word out in an unpleasant way.

"The wear-in."

She came toward him. Her head was turned to the side as if she had heard wrong out of her left ear and was giving her right one a chance.

"Run that by me again," she said.

Bingo got up from the chair and moved behind it. He took two steps backward toward the dining room.

"You know, last night, at the table? Remember you said we should rebel and have a wear-in, and that I should be the leader? Well, I can't be the leader—I'm sorry, I'm just not up to

70

it. I honestly tried, but you know me."
He gave an apologetic shrug.

His mom kept coming.

"But it's not off. You know the boy who's moving next door? Billy Wentworth? He's leading it. He got up on the school trash can to announce it and—"

"Wait a minute. Wait—a—minute."

Bingo waited, but not happily.

"You told this boy, this Wentworth boy, that I had suggested a school rebellion?"

Bingo struggled for a better way to put it. For the first time in his life he felt the nickname *Worm Brain* might be right. His mother took his silence for a yes.

"Well, that is the end, the absolute end."

She looked up at the ceiling. She took several deep breaths to calm herself, but it didn't work. When she looked down at Bingo again, her eyes were as cold as those of the President of the United States.

"Have you ever heard," she asked, in a voice to match the deep-freeze eyes, "of tongue-in-cheek."

"No, no, what is it?"

"Have you ever heard of humor, of saying something to be funny?"

"Yes, yes, I've heard of that."

Now she said nothing. She breathed. Bingo would not have been surprised if fire had started coming out of her nose.

He couldn't stand it. He grabbed the only way out—something he resorted to only when he was absolutely desperate—the lie.

"Oh, Mom, Mom! Listen, I didn't say you personally suggested it. I just said, like, 'It would be nice if we protested,' something like that. No, here are my exact words, I just remembered. My exact words were, 'Oh, I hope we don't rebel.' And he said, 'How could we?' I said, 'I don't know, maybe a wear-in day where everybody wears an illegal shirt.' "

Bingo had to swallow a lot of spit before he could continue. "I certainly have enough sense not to involve you. After all, you *are* Secretary of the PTA. I would never involve you in anything that would cast dispersions on your officership."

She folded her arms over her chest. "If you are lying to me, Harrison—" His mom only called him by his real name in moments like this.

Bingo made an X on his chest to indicate truth, a big one that covered his entire chest and both his hips.

"So." She began breathing more normally. "When is the wear-in going to be and what are you going to wear?"

"Friday and Mozart Freak. It's the only thing clean." He didn't think it was the moment to apologize for not having PRINCIPALS STINK.

"Good choice."

Relief, Bingo decided, was the most wonderful emotion in the world.

"Thank you," he said. "Well, I'll be going now."

Bingo backed out of the kitchen,

down the hall, and into his room, wiping well-earned sweat from his brow.

By the next morning, Bingo was back to normal. He joined the students of Roosevelt Middle School outside the building.

No one was thinking of going inside. Everyone was talking about the wear-in. The girls were in clusters, planning which of their shirts would be most appropriate.

Bingo moved from group to group, happily eavesdropping. Naturally Billy was going to wear Rambo, but he had bought a brand-new Rambo shirt. That was a sign of the importance he himself placed on the day.

Bingo had assumed that Mamie Lou would wear BEACH BOYS, but she was not. She said it didn't have enough words on it. She was going to wear one that said IF YOU CAN READ THIS YOU ARE TOO CLOSE. Although this did not make Bingo fall back in love with her, it did make him think of her as presidential material again.

George Rogers was wearing WEIRD BUT LOVABLE.

Hughie McManus was wearing SHUD UPPA U FACE.

Freddie was wearing I ARE A GENIUS.

Amy Myers was wearing IN A WORLD FULL OF COPIES, HERE'S AN ORIGINAL.

Marian Wong was wearing HAVE YOU THANKED A PLANT TODAY?

Harriet was wearing SMASH COMPUTERS AND LET THE CHIPS FALL WHERE THEY MAY.

And Melissa! Now he was truly, hopelessly in love. Melissa was borrowing a shirt from her mom. On this shirt was printed the entire Declaration of Independence. Her mother—Bingo overheard Melissa telling Harriet this —wore the shirt whenever she'd absolutely had it with everybody in the family. Whenever the family saw her in this shirt, they backed off.

Bingo had the feeling that tomorrow was going to be the most wonderful day of his life. He went into the school with everyone else. He had only one question. What could spoil this perfect day?

Mr. Markham was sitting at his desk, looking as if he had the answer to Bingo's question. His eyes were not closed, but there was something about his expression that made them stop talking about t-shirts.

"Is anything wrong, Mr. Mark?" Melissa asked.

"You tell me. Sit down, gang."

They sat.

Mr. Markham stared down at his desk for one minute and then looked up. This was effective. Bingo had the feeling Mr. Markham was going to say something about the poor quality of the Dawn letters. Bingo looked down at his desk.

Mr. Markham said, "In case any of you are planning to wear shirts tomorrow with words on them—" He paused. This was also effective. Bingo looked up. "—don't!"

The class sat without moving. All

morning they had been in a blaze of unified excitement. Many of them already had their illegal shirts laid out on their beds at home. Many of them planned to wear the shirts to sleep.

Madame President said, "Why?" She was too upset to go through the ritual of holding up her hand.

"Mr. Boehmer will be at the door," Mr. Markham said, "and the reason he will be there is so that he can personally inspect every student and send home anyone who is wearing a shirt with writing on it of any kind."

Bingo had a rush of unmanly questions. *Could I wear a jacket tomorrow? Could I go in the side door? Could I be tardy? Could I—*

Billy Wentworth put up his hand.

Mr. Markham said, "Yes, Billy?"

"What time?"

"What time what?"

"What time will Boehmer be at the door?"

"Oh, eight o'clock."

"Tell him something for me."

77

"What?"

"Tell him I'll be waiting for him."

Bingo was electrified. This was the boy he didn't want to live next door to! This hero! This man in a boy's disguise! It would be a privilege and an honor to live next door to Billy Wentworth.

An awed silence followed Billy's announcement. Then the class began to clap.

"Gang," Mr. Markham said, "there is no reason to applaud anarchy."

They kept clapping.

"Gang!"

Still they clapped.

"Look, I'm not going to be here to bail you out. I'm going to be out of town tomorrow. You're going to have a substitute."

They were going to keep clapping until they wore out their hands. Nothing could stop them. Nothing!

Only one thing.

Billy Wentworth put his fingers to

his throat and gave them the signal to cut it.

They cut.

TOMORROW, ABOUT 8:05

"OH, BY the way," Bingo said casually at the supper table.

"Not now, Bingo," his mom said. "Your dad's talking. Why can't you go to homecoming, Sam? This is terrible."

"Mr. Richardson wants me to go to Lima, Ohio, and give a presentation."

"Didn't you tell him it was homecoming?"

"Yes."

"Didn't he care?"

"Not really."

"Well, if you don't go, I'm not going either."

"Of course you'll go. You've been practicing 'Fight, Darn You, Fight' for weeks."

Actually she had only been practicing for two days, but it seemed like weeks.

"It wouldn't be fun without you."

"You have to go. You were the best trumpet player they had."

"I'll think about it."

"You mean you really would go without me?"

"I didn't say that. I said I'd think about it."

There was a silence, and Bingo filled it with, "Oh, by the way, I may be home from school early tomorrow."

His mom said, "What time?"

"Eight-oh-five."

The very casual delivery of the answer had the desired effect. Both parents stopped eating and looked at him. Bingo chewed his food slowly, the way his mom was always urging him to do.

"We're having our protest wear-in tomorrow," he said. He started a new shish kebab. "Mr. Boehmer, the principal, is going to stand at the front door of the school. At eight-oh-five he is going to personally inspect every student and send home anyone who has on a t-shirt with writing on it." He waved his fork in a figure-eight. "Needless to say, I and every other red-blooded student in Roosevelt Middle School will have on such shirts and will be sent home."

He put his food in his mouth. While he chewed, his parents had time to register doubts about the wisdom of a rebellion. It could go on his permanent record. *Participation in Middle-School Rebellion,* would not look good.

But they couldn't help themselves. They were too proud. Bingo could see their pride in the way they inflated themselves with air. They didn't inflate like that very often.

"What does Mr. Markham have to say about all of this?" his mother asked after she had deflated.

"Nothing."

"Nothing? His students are in the middle of a rebellion and he has no comment?"

"He said we shouldn't applaud anarchy and he said he was going to be out of town and wouldn't be able to bail us out. That was about it."

"You like Mr. Markham, don't you?"

"Sure. Why wouldn't I?"

"I don't know. I've heard varying reports."

Bingo stopped making his shish kebab. "Like what?"

"Nothing specific. Some parents feel he isn't," she paused to find the right word, "let's say *stable*."

"Nobody's stable," Bingo said. "Even I am not perfectly stable."

"Oh, really?" She smiled. "Well, maybe *stable* was the wrong word. It was just little things, like last year he had students write letters persuading some girl to go out with him."

"Well, we've never done that," Bingo answered truthfully. "Anyway, he does stuff like that to make life interesting. What do you want him to assign—*My Summer Vacation?*"

"No."

"I should think you'd be glad I have a teacher I like for a change."

"I am."

"And that I am taking an active part in school politics."

"I am."

"Then," Bingo said, "you should act like it."

"Bravo, Bingo," his father said.

Sleep, of course, was out of the question that night because he was so thrilled over the wear-in. Friday was shaping up to be the biggest day of his entire life.

There was only one worry. Since it was the biggest day of his life, he wasn't sure he wanted to spend it in a shirt that said MOZART FREAK.

To be honest, he had worn that shirt at least once a week all last year, and he had started off the fall in it as well. MOZART FREAK wasn't special any more. Certainly it was not worthy of Melissa's Declaration of Independence. Nor of Harriet's shirt. He had learned that afternoon that Harriet was wearing a shirt with dolphins on the front and underneath were the words I HAVE A PORPOISE IN LIFE.

Bingo tossed and turned. His Snoopy sheets became twisted and sweaty.

He got up at eleven, put on the light, and went through his bureau drawers, thinking that perhaps he had a shirt he'd forgotten about. He got up again at twelve. This time he went to his mom's room and quietly opened her t-shirt drawer.

"What are you doing, Bingo?" she asked, lifting her head off the pillow.

"Nothing, Mom, go back to sleep."

"What are you doing in my bureau drawer?"

"Nothing, Mom, just checking out your t-shirts."

"At midnight?"

"Mom, everybody is wearing these great t-shirts tomorrow and I'm stuck with Mozart Freak. I've got to have something better. I've got to!"

"Well, you should have thought of that before midnight. Go back to bed."

"Mom—"

"Go to bed, Bingo!" This was his father's command-voice.

"Yes, sir."

Bingo went to bed, but he couldn't sleep. About one o'clock he made a decision. He would *create* a t-shirt. He would take a blank t-shirt, and he would write WORDS on it. That would be all, except that the O would be the not-allowed symbol: Ø.

He got out of bed. Unfortunately, the only blank t-shirts were in his father's underwear drawer. Silently Bingo crept into his parents' room, silently opened the drawer, withdrew the top t-shirt, and departed.

On the way back to his room, he slipped through the house, gathering Magic Markers from various drawers. In order to insure that the shirt was colorful, he was going to make each letter a different color. The Ø would be red.

Bingo set to work. As soon as he started he was electrified. The shirt was going to be beautiful, beautiful, and best of all was the fact that he hadn't put cardboard inside the shirt before he started and so now the color was going through the material.

At last Bingo was finished. He draped his t-shirt over his dresser so that the first thing he would see in the morning was WØRDS. He stood for moment admiring the letters, the coloring, the—

"Bingo, are you still up?"

"No."

"Then why is your light on?"

"I mean, yes, I'm up, but I'm going to bed right now."

Bingo turned off the light. He fell across his crumpled Snoopy sheets. At last he was ready for the most thrilling day of his life.

THE MOST THRILLING DAY OF BINGO BROWN'S LIFE

"WHAT DO you think?"

Bingo stood in the doorway to the kitchen in his WØRDS t-shirt. His parents put down their coffee cups and turned to look at him.

"Be honest now."

"I thought you had decided to wear Mozart Freak," his mom said.

"Mom, I told you last night it wasn't special enough. Wait, you haven't seen the back." he turned slowly, revealing SDRØW. "Now what do you think?"

Many of his past creations had looked good on paper but had not worked out—like last Halloween. The disguise was perfect, but it took him a half hour to walk to the first house. *This* had worked out.

There was another long pause.

Finally his dad said, "It's different."

"Really? You aren't just saying that?"

His mom said, "Your dad's right. There won't be another one like it."

"Thanks."

"Now sit down and have some breakfast."

"Mom, I can't eat. I've got to get to school!"

"Bingo, it won't take five minutes to eat a bowl of cereal."

"Mom, I'm late already. Everybody's going to be there early, to get a good place. If I'm late, I'll miss it." The thought of that brought such anguish that he turned immediately and started for the door.

"Bingo, it's not even seven o'clock yet, now come back here and—"

The slamming of the front door was her answer.

Every single person was already at school when Bingo got there. Every single person was wearing a t-shirt with something written on it. The schoolyard was ablaze with words. It was a dictionary come to life.

HELP, I'M BEING HELD PRISONER IN THIS SHIRT!

AVAILABLE FOR CLONING.

I AM SURROUNDED BY IDIOTS.

ARCHEOLOGY IS THE PITS.

ONLY LEFT-HANDED PEOPLE ARE IN THEIR RIGHT MIND.

Bingo had never enjoyed anything so much. His mouth hung open in admiration.

NOTICE: THE AREA BEHIND THIS SHIRT IS PROTECTED UNDER THE ENDANGERED SPECIES ACT.

I HAVE SOMETHING MONEY CAN'T BUY—POVERTY.

RANIUM—THE ONLY THING MISSING IS U.

COMPUTER CHIPS ARE SMALL BECAUSE COMPUTERS TAKE SMALL BYTES.

CAUTION: I KNOW KARATE AND A FEW OTHER ORIENTAL WORDS.

BE ALERT—THE WORLD NEEDS MORE LERTS.

SPLIT WOOD—NOT ATOMS.

STOP CONTINENTAL DRIFT.

BEAM ME UP SCOTTY. THERE IS NO INTEL-LIGENT LIFE DOWN HERE.

REALITY IS FOR THOSE WHO CAN'T FACE SCIENCE FICTION.

π^2 NO! PI ARE ROUND. CAKE ARE SQUARE.

Bingo's long wandering path among his classmates brought him to the steps of the school. Billy Wentworth stood there alone, head and shoulders above the crowd. His eyes looked at some distant spot on the horizon.

He had on his newly purchased Rambo t-shirt. His combat boots and camouflage pants completed the outfit. His hands were behind his back. He was standing at what Bingo recognized from war movies as Parade Rest. He would draw an aerial view of it later in his journal.

Below him, the students milled around the schoolyard, admiring t-shirts and shivering with excitement and the chill of the fall morning. The October air was charged with electricity.

YOU QUACK ME UP.

DON'T BUG ME. THIS IS MY DO-NOTHING T-SHIRT!

I'M NOT OVERWEIGHT—I'M UNDERTALL.

HERE I COME . . . THERE I GO.

It was a measure of their excitement and dedication that not one of them had thought to bring books, homework, or lunches. These items no longer had any meaning. They were *wearing* the only items of lasting value.

The time ticked slowly by . . . seven-thirty . . . seven-forty. "What time is it now?" the kids without watches kept asking. Ten minutes to eight . . . five minutes to eight . . .

When eight o'clock came, Billy Wentworth shifted position. He stopped Parade Rest and turned sharply to face the front door.

As if on signal, the kids closed in around him. The only sounds were the coughs of the sick kids who had come to school anyway. "Mom, I'm just going for five minutes," they had told their moms. Some of the moms were waiting across the street in station wagons, motors idling, so they could rush the invalids back to bed.

At eight-oh-five there was a metallic sound. The inside doors were being unlocked.

Roosevelt Middle School had two sets of doors. There were inside doors and then there was a little room which was never used, and then the outside doors. So there was going to be a lot of door unlocking before the main event.

The inside doors had now been opened. Bingo could see the shadow of a man in the room that was never used. The shadow moved toward the outside doors.

Bingo's heart moved up into his throat. He had stopped breathing a long time ago.

Billy Wentworth was the only person in motion, and all he did was wipe his hands on the back of his camouflage pants as if he were getting ready for a fight.

Everyone on the school ground was frozen in place. Bingo was sandwiched between Melissa in her Declaration of Independence and Harriet in her I HAVE A PORPOISE IN LIFE, but he didn't even notice he was between his two loves, didn't even feel the warmth of their shoulders against his.

Now the outside doors were being unlocked. Now they were being opened.

No one breathed. No one moved.

A figure appeared in the doorway, a figure in a gray jumpsuit. It was the janitor! *The janitor!* THE JANITOR!

Their mouths dropped open. They blinked their eyes to clear their vision, and it was still THE JANITOR.

Now everybody started looking around at everybody else. The exact same burning questions were popped in every mind.

What's going on here?

Where's Boehmer?

What's the janitor doing opening the doors?

How can this be the most thrilling day of our lives if Boehmer and Billy

Wentworth don't have a head-to-head confrontation?

Bingo briefly considered leading the crowd in a chant. *We want Boehmer! We want Boehmer!* Maybe he had gotten his father's cheerleading gene after all.

Before he could put this plan into effect, however, Billy Wentworth turned around. He locked his hands over his head and gave the victory signal.

Through the sudden tears in Bingo's eyes, he saw Billy Wentworth disappear through the outside doors, into the little room which was never used, through the inside doors and into the school.

Then he didn't have to lead the crowd. They burst into a rousing cry that could be heard five miles away.

"YYYYYYYYEEEEEEEEAAAAA-AAAAHHHHHHH!"

And then in a rush, they happily followed their rebel leader inside.

BINGO'S EMBRACE

BINGO HAD thought that his thrills were over for the day when he walked into the classroom and saw the substitute teacher.

"My name's Miss Brownley," a lady with a bushel-basket of hair said, "and I'm your substitute for the day."

Mamie Lou put up her hand. "Miss Brownley?"

"Yes."

"Where's Mr. Boehmer?"

"The principal? I believe he had a staff meeting this morning. He'll be in his office later."

"Why wasn't he at the door?"

"What door?"

"The front door! He was supposed to be at the front door! We weren't supposed to wear shirts with writing on them and we did and he was supposed to send us home but he didn't. Why?"

"I have no idea," said Miss Brownley.

Yes, Bingo thought, the thrills were over for the day. Then at exactly ten twenty-three something happened that made the wear-in seem like child's play. Melissa walked into his arms.

This was the first time that Melissa and Bingo had ever made real contact so Bingo would have been pleased even if their hands had bumped or she had stepped on his tennis shoe. To have her walk into his arms was like something out of a soap opera. It left him delirious.

The embrace came about in an unexpected way. To get the class to calm down, Miss Brownley asked them to write in their journals.

Everyone was too excited to think of something to write. Even Bingo had no burning questions.

"Let me make a suggestion," Miss Brownley said. "Write about someone who has significantly changed your life—a teacher, a coach, perhaps one of your parents. It could even be someone on television . . ."

While Miss Brownley droned on, Bingo wrote a page and a half about the doctor who had been responsible for his being named Bingo. He ended with a question. *Who knows what kind of person I might have become had the doctor said, "Richard!" instead of "Bingo!"*

He illustrated the piece with a picture of the doctor holding up the unfortunate baby. Even with all that, he was finished before anybody else. He immediately broke his pencil.

Bingo felt safe in doing this. Usually he didn't break his pencil until he made it to the pencil sharpener, but Miss Brownley was new and had never seen him in action before.

He took his time getting to the pencil sharpener and leisurely checked out the people who had significantly changed the lives of his classmates.

No one's lives had been changed very significantly. There was a kindergarten teacher called Miss Tiffany. A Little League coach. Mr. Rogers . . .

Then Bingo got to Melissa's desk. Melissa was bending over her paper. The long sleeves of her Declaration of Independence t-shirt blocked his view.

Then she lifted her arm and—to Bingo's horror—she wiped her eyes with her sleeve. Melissa was crying!

Bingo drew in a deep breath of concern.

Melissa started writing again, but a tear fell onto her page. She tried to write over the tear, but she bore down on her pencil and the point broke.

Now Bingo saw the reason for the tears. Melissa was writing about her father, and Melissa's father was unemployed.

Bingo stood there, aching with sympathy, ready to cry himself. At that moment, blinded by her tears, Melissa jumped up to go to the pencil sharpener, and she plunged directly into Bingo's waiting arms.

"Excuse me," she gasped.

"Of course, of course."

She tried to go around him and he

tried to get out of her way, but they both went in the same direction and embraced again.

"I'm sorry," she gasped.

"Me too." Then Bingo said manfully, "Here. Let me." He took the pencil from her and she sank back in her seat. It seemed a grateful sink to Bingo.

He stepped to the pencil sharpener and then proceeded to do the second most thrilling thing he had ever done in his life. He sharpened Melissa's pencil.

It was so rewarding that he kept sharpening and sharpening. He would have sharpened down to the eraser except that Miss Brownley said, "Bingo."

"What?"

"I didn't give you permission to go to the pencil sharpener."

"Oh, sorry, Miss Brownley. I didn't know we had to have permission. Mr. Mark just lets us use our own judgment."

"Class, while I'm here, I'd like for

you to ask permission to leave your desks."

"I will next time. Anyway, I'm sharpening Melissa's pencil right now. Afterwards, I'll be—"

"Isn't Melissa capable of sharpening her own pencil?"

"Yes," Bingo said gallantly, "but since I was already up and she was down—"

"Bingo, I don't want to have to send you to the principal's office."

Bingo stopped being gallant. Mr. Boehmer had not been seen all morning, and so the first student his eyes would fall on would be Bingo. The first shirt his eyes would see would say WØRDS, a cruel reminder of his morning cowardice.

"I am going to my desk at once," Bingo said. He turned to Melissa. "Here," he said and presented the pencil.

"Thanks, Bingo."

His name! She said his name! He loved his name the way she said it!

He then returned to his desk. Even Mr. Markham could have found no fault with the purposeful way he walked. He didn't check out a single paper. At his desk, he turned smartly and took his seat.

It was then that he discovered he had forgotten to sharpen his own pencil, but what was that compared with holding Melissa and the Declaration of Independence in his arms?

Friday night's supper was one of the best Bingo could remember. Every member of the family had something to be happy about.

Bingo was the happiest. He had double triumphs—the wear-in and the embrace. His father was next happiest because someone named Mr. Kroll was going to Lima, Ohio. Now he could be standing on his hands with the other cheerleaders. His mom was third happiest because now she did not have to decide whether to go to homecoming without him.

"Would you have gone without me?" Bingo's father asked.

"I might have, because I told them I would and they're counting on my trumpet."

"Oh."

"But I wouldn't have enjoyed it. You know that."

Bingo said, "Isn't anyone going to ask about the wear-in?"

"I am," his mom said. "I'm dying to hear about the wear-in. How did it go?"

"It was a triumph. Boehmer never showed up. He was too chicken. He pretended to be in a staff meeting."

"Maybe he *was* in a staff meeting."

"Mom, don't be naive. Billy Wentworth led us into the school and Boehmer hid out in the office all day. Billy Wentworth—he's the boy that's moving next door—was—"

"Oh, speaking of homecoming," his mom interrupted. "Now that we're going for sure, I better call Mom and see if she can stay with Bingo. I'll call after supper."

This was more good news. Bingo loved his grandmother. She was like his mother in looks, except a little more wrinkled. She and his mom wore the same size and borrowed each other's clothes. They both wore their hair pulled back. There was only one difference, really. Bingo's grandmother was perfect. She did not have one fault.

She let him have what he wanted to eat. She let him do what he wanted to do. She loved to take him to the movies. She loved to make popcorn for him. She made pancakes in the shapes of animals.

She said, "Why, of course you do," all the time. Like Bingo would say, "I want ice cream on my cornflakes."

"Why, of course you do."

Splat.

Also his grandmother called him by his real name—Harrison—which was very refreshing after all the Bingos.

"When are you going exactly?" he

asked. A weekend of having every single one of his wishes—no matter how foolish—fulfilled, would do a lot for him.

"Two weeks from today."

That night should have been a peaceful one for Bingo. Not only had it been a perfect day, but his mom had changed the sheets on his bed. He always slept well on his Smurf sheets.

But as soon as he closed his eyes, a question came.

If it had been Harriet who walked into my arms in her I HAVE A PORPOISE IN LIFE *shirt, would it have been (a) as thrilling, (b) more thrilling, or (c) not thrilling at all?*

NEW MEANING TO LIFE

THE ONLY noteworthy event of Monday was that Miss Brownley personally walked around the classroom, putting pink slips of paper on everyone's desk.

104

"You are to take these home, boys and girls, and have one of your parents sign them."

The pink slips said, *Yes, my child has permission to wear printed t-shirts to Roosevelt Middle School and I will take full responsibility for any words or messages thereon.* There was a blank below for the signature.

"Miss Brownley?"

"Yes, Mamie Lou."

"I thought Mr. Markham was going to be back today."

"I think he had planned to be back today, but there was some sort of problem."

"What was the problem?"

"I couldn't say."

"Does that mean that you know the problem and won't tell us what it is? Or does it mean you don't know the problem?"

Miss Brownley gave her a look instead of an answer.

"Can I ask you one more thing, Miss Brownley?"

"You can ask."

"Does it have anything to do with Dawn?"

"I couldn't say."

Bingo spent most of Monday trying to put meaning back into his life. This was essential because after the thrill of the wear-in and the embrace, the rest of his life seemed unimportant.

He sat listlessly at his desk. Even Math—which he liked—had no meaning. Instead of multiplying like the rest of the class, he found himself asking 174 whats? 2498 whats? In a desperate effort to give meaning to the numbers, he began illustrating his problems, but even that—174 oranges times 2495 apples equals 434,652 mixed fruits—didn't seem to work.

A second embrace from Melissa would have helped a lot, but even though he made several trips to the pencil sharpener, giving her every opportunity to jump up, she had not done so. This was especially disappointing since he had worked out a plan to go directly from Melissa's arms to Harriet's desk where he would yell something like, "Spider!"

Harriet would leap up in alarm. His arms would be waiting. They would embrace and he would know the truth.

During Math, he decided to try again. He put up his hand.

"What now, Bingo?"

"I seem to have broken my pencil again."

Miss Brownley said, "Will someone lend Bingo a pencil?"

"My mom doesn't like me to borrow. She—"

"I have an extra pencil," Mamie Lou said. "Pass that back to Bingo."

The pencil was not quite an inch long. It was an eraser with a point on it.

"What if I break this pencil?"

"You won't."

"Miss Brownley—"

"Bingo, I have been keeping a record of the number of times you have been to the pencil sharpener, and in the day and a half that I have been substituting for Mr. Markham, you have been to the pencil sharpener nine times."

"It can't be that many—two or three maybe. I know I break a lot of pencils, Miss Brownley, I can't help it. I bear down hard."

She held up a notepad. On the pad were nine marks. She had been keeping a record!

"If you would like me to," she went on, "I'll be happy to write your mother a note, stating the problem, and requesting additional pencils."

"That won't be necessary," Bingo said firmly. "I'll make this one last."

"Good."

He did the rest of his math problems in pale, meaningless numbers, sparing the lead of his pencil. When he wrote in his journal, he wrote in pale letters only one question.

Is my life as a happy person over?

It was Billy Wentworth who put meaning back into Bingo's life. He did it with one sentence.

"I'm moving next door to you Saturday."

"Saturday?"

"That's what I said, Worm Brain. Saturday."

With that single statement, the enormity of the occasion washed over Bingo like a tidal wave. He would get to see what kind of furniture a hero had. He would see the refrigerator his food went in. He would see his chairs. He would see Billy Wentworth's bed!

"Bingo."

"What have I done now, Miss Brownley?" Had he gone to the pencil sharpener without knowing it—like a sleepwalker? "I honestly don't know what I've done."

"You were staring into space."

"Oh." Had she been keeping a record of his staring-into-spaces too? He would be glad to have Mr. Markham back. Even writing letters to Dawn was better than this.

Mr. Markham came back the next day in time to collect the pink slips.

"I forgot mine, Mr. Mark," Bingo said. "I've had a lot on my mind lately."

"I'm glad to hear that, Bingo—that you have something on your mind."

Mr. Markham sounded like the old Mr. Mark, but he looked smaller, as if he was wearing his big brother's clothes.

"Mr. Mark?"

"Yes, Mamie Lou."

"You missed the wear-in. You didn't get to see us in our shirts."

"I was with you in spirit."

"I wanted you to see us."

Mr. Markham put the pink slips in his desk drawer. "Hey, that gives me an idea, gang. Let's start off with Art. We haven't had Art in weeks. Get out a piece of paper and draw a picture of yourself in your t-shirt. We'll put the pictures up on the board as a reminder of your daring. Yes, Melissa?"

"My shirt had the whole Declaration of Independence on it. I'm not sure I remember it word for word."

"Fake it."

Everyone began work at once. The pictures had been burned into their brains since Friday, and it was a relief to be able to recreate them.

Mr. Markham stood at the window, looking out. There wasn't much out there—the parking lot and the side of the gymnasium, but Mr. Markham kept looking until they finished the pictures. Melissa said, "Mr. Mark, we're through with the pictures."

He turned around then. "Pictures? Yes, pictures. Melissa, would you take down the harvest display from the bulletin board and organize the t-shirt display?"

"Sure."

Bingo was grateful to Mr. Markham for the display. He glanced sideways at it all during the week.

The pictures were better than photographs. Harriet in I HAVE A PORPOISE IN LIFE. Billy in Rambo. Melissa in what appeared to be the complete Declaration of Independence. Barbara in the

Statue of Liberty—ANY HUNDRED-YEAR-OLD LADY NEEDS A LIFT NOW AND THEN. Bingo in WØRDS.

Being watched over by pictures of themselves at their best did something for all of them. Billy drew no weaponry. Bingo did not go to the pencil sharpener. They were so quiet that Mr. Markham only had to close his eyes once.

When Bingo wrote in his journal on Friday, his questions reflected the peaceful nature of the week.

Is this the way my life is going to be from now on?

Am I at last in a period of peace?

Is this adulthood?

Or is this what's known as the calm that comes before the storm?

Will Billy Wentworth have bunk beds?

SPYING ON A SUPERSTAR

"COME AWAY from the window and stop spying on the Wentworths."

Bingo snapped the curtains shut and spun around. "I was not spying."

"Bingo Brown, you've been spying ever since you got up."

"I have not. I've done dozens of things since I got up."

"You have done exactly two things. One, run to the window. Two, spy. Look at you. You aren't even dressed. You're still in your pajamas."

Bingo sighed. He could see that this was one of the times he was not going to change his mom's mind, no matter how hard he tried. Her specialty was false accusations.

He decided to do what his mother and the President of the United States did in similar situations—turn icy.

He said coldly, "Would I be accused of further spying if I went to my room? After all, my room does face the Wentworths' house. If my eyes happen to glance out my own window, would you call this spying too?"

"Yes."

"Mom!"

"You asked me."

"Well, I didn't expect you to answer like that. You don't have to hurt my feelings. You should—"

His mom reached out and took his shoulder. She said, "Look."

"What? Where?"

"They've got a wide-screen TV."

"Where? Let me see. Mom, I want to see too."

They jostled for position at the window and ended up with Bingo in front and his mom peering over his head. In silence they watched the wide-screen TV being carried up the stairs. The men had to turn it sideways to get it in the front door.

"They're probably going to put it in the living room," his mom said. "If they were putting it in the game room, they'd take it in through the garage, don't you think? Can you see where they're putting it?"

"I could if you'd move over, Mom, and let me stand up straight."

"With a wide-screen TV, the father's probably into sports."

"Bowling," Bingo said.

"How do you know it's bowling? You don't need a wide screen to watch bowling."

"Well, he went to a roast for one of his bowling buddies, I know that for a fact."

"Is that a Jenn-Air stove? I—" The phone rang then and Bingo's mom said, "Get that for me, Bingo?"

"Why should I get it? It's never for me."

"Oh, all right."

Bingo kept watching until his mom came back. "You missed the stereo. It was—"

"The phone," his mother announced, "is for you."

"Me?"

"It's a girl."

"For me?"

"Your name is Bingo, isn't it?"

Bingo went to the phone slowly. This was the first time he had ever talked to a girl on the phone, and he was not sure he was ready for a mixed-sex conversation. He took a deep breath and picked up the phone. He held it away from his head so it didn't touch him.

"Hello."

"Bingo?"

"Yes, it's me. Who is this?"

"Melissa."

"Melissa!"

"Yes. Hi. Bingo, can I talk to you for a minute?"

"Sure."

"Because I've just got to talk to somebody. I can't keep this to myself any longer."

"What? What is it?"

Bingo sank down onto the chair. His heart had started to pound. This was the way mixed-sex conversations were supposed to be—intriguing, mysterious—only Bingo had never thought of himself as having one. He brought the phone closer.

"Bingo, do you remember the other

day when Mr. Mark made us write letters to Dawn?"

This was not what Bingo was expecting, but he said quickly, "I remember that."

"Remember he made me get up and describe her?"

"Yes, I remember. You did a good job too."

Melissa sighed.

"What's wrong?"

She sighed again. Bingo got to his feet in alarm. Was it something he had said? Was it something he had not said? He would say anything she wanted him to, didn't she know that?

"Well, remember I said Mr. Mark went in the store and she stayed outside?"

"Yes, yes."

"Remember I said I went over and said, 'Hi'?"

"Yes, yes."

"I just did it to be friendly. She said, 'Hi,' back to me. Then she said,

'What's your name?' I said, 'Melissa.' She said, 'Mine's Dawn.' "

There was a long pause. Bingo wondered if that was the end of the conversation. He didn't want to say, "Well, I'm glad we had this talk," in case there was more. On the other hand, he *was* glad to have had this talk. It was the best mixed-sex conversation he had ever had in his life.

"That's not all," Melissa said as if she had read his mind. Bingo sank slowly back into the chair.

"I said, 'Are you and Mr. Mark going somewhere special? I'm in his room at school.' I said that because I didn't want her to think I was just being nosy."

"Oh."

"She said, 'We're going on a picnic.' I said, 'Oh, neat. I love picnics.' She said, 'Well, I don't. He came by the spa where I work and offered me a ride home. At first I said no, but then he promised to take me straight home so I got on. Right away he U-turned and brought me here. I can't go on a picnic. I told him that but he won't listen. Now he's gone in the store to get hotdogs.' "

Bingo had never realized before what a good conversationalist Melissa was. He had known she was beautiful and intelligent and sensitive, but she was so good at imitating people that he knew exactly how Dawn sounded.

"So I said, 'Are you his girlfriend?' She was so nice I felt like I could ask her anything. And she said, 'No, I could never be his girlfriend because he's too erratic, like this picnic that I don't want to go on. I've got a date tonight and he probably won't take me home in time to get ready.' Then she looked around and said, 'I wish I could see somebody I knew,' and then she looked at me and said, 'Oh, could I get a ride home with you? Where's your car—quick?' Before I could answer, Mr. Mark came out of the store. She said, 'Oh, there he is. I could just cry.' "

There was a long pause, and then Melissa said, "That's all."

"Oh?"

"That was all the conversation. They got on the bike and drove off."

"Oh." Bingo was trying to put a lot of variety in his Oh's, making each one different.

"I wanted to tell somebody about it because it made me feel terrible the other day when he said she was his girlfriend. She's not his girlfriend. I don't even think she likes him."

"Oh."

"I wish I had her last name so I could call her up."

"Me too."

"Anyway, you know something?"

"What?"

"Just telling you about it has made me feel better."

"Oh."

"Thanks for listening."

"I was glad to."

"Bye."

He went slowly back to the window.

"You missed the bunk beds, two La-Z-Boy recliners and a beanbag chair," his mom said.

"Oh."

"Here they come! The Wentworths and the kids."

Bingo watched as the car drove up and stopped in front of the house. Billy got out of the car, then his sister—they were having an argument. The sister was saying, "I got the big bedroom because I take care of things. You are a slob." There was a bumper sticker on the car that said I'D RATHER BE BOWLING.

Also, Bingo had sort of lost interest. A good mixed-sex conversation made bunk beds and beanbag chairs unimportant. Plus he had gotten a mental picture of how he might look to Billy Wentworth.

And then Bingo stepped up to the window. He gasped with surprise. He threw open the curtain.

For at that moment, getting out of the car along with the family, was the most unbelievable sight Bingo had ever seen, something he had not dreamed could be true, something he would remember for the rest of his life.

Billy Wentworth had a poodle.

THE WORST NEWS OF BINGO'S LIFE

BINGO WAS walking home slowly. This was because he had just had another mixed-sex conversation.

Melissa had said, "Can I speak to you after school?"

"Sure, sure."

"It's about what I told you on the phone."

"All right."

The second mixed-sex conversation was held on the school steps. Melissa said, "After I talked to you, I started thinking."

"Yes, yes."

"Maybe Dawn wasn't Mr. Markham's girlfriend when I talked to her,

122

but maybe she got to be his girlfriend after that. See what I mean?"

"I think so."

"After I thought about that, I wanted to call you back because I was afraid I had made you worry about Mr. Mark like I was worrying about Mr. Mark, but I was afraid to call you back because I was afraid your mom would answer and she would think I was calling you too much."

"You can call me anytime you want to."

"Really? You mean that?"

"Yes."

Bingo was replaying the conversation in his mind when he rounded the corner, so he did not immediately recognize the awful sound that filled the street. Then he recognized it and broke into a run.

"Mom!" He threw open the living room door. "Stop! Don't!" he cried.

"Don't what?"

"Play the trumpet."

"Why?"

"They'll hear you."

"Who?"

"The Wentworths."

"The Wentworths have heard trumpet-playing before. Anyway, this is when people are supposed to practice—in the middle of the afternoon when nobody's trying to sleep."

"Couldn't you at least play it quietly? Aren't there mutes or something you can stick in trumpets to make them quiet?"

"Fight songs are not minuets, Bingo. You're supposed to give them all you've got. Now let go of my arm."

"Can I at least close the window?"

"I want to get used to playing outside—oh, all right, close the window and I'll go out in the yard."

"No! Not the yard! The window's fine."

"Well, make up your mind."

Bingo walked into his room with one question in his mind.

In the morning at school, could he say to Billy, "Man, did you hear that

124

terrible trumpet-playing yesterday? Somebody stinks"?

Would Billy answer, "Yeah, and it's your mom"?

While he was lying on the bed, trying to get his mind to return to the mixed-sex conversation, his mom came into the room.

"Oh, about homecoming—"

"What about it?" Bingo said without interest. In his mind Melissa had just said the opening word in the mixed-sex conversation. *Bingo.*

"Well, Mom's not going to be able to stay with you. This is her bridge weekend. You know, once a year she and her seven best friends go to a resort hotel and play bridge all weekend. They've been doing it since 1965. Last year she had to miss because of her gallbladder, and I couldn't ask her to miss again. This year they're going to the Myrtle Beach Holiday Inn."

"So what am I going to do?"

"Well, this falls under the heading of a stroke of luck. I went over to the

Wentworths to introduce myself and while we were talking, I mentioned the weekend and that I didn't have anyone for you to stay with, and she said, 'Why, he can stay with us. Billy has an extra bunk bed.' I really like her. She is so nice. I—"

Bingo sat straight up in bed. "Mom," he said, his voice was firm, adult, and controlled except that it was four notes higher than usual. "Mom, I cannot spend the night with Billy Wentworth."

"But why? He seems like such a nice boy."

"I cannot explain it but you'll just have to believe me, Mom. I cannot spend the night with Billy Wentworth."

"But why? Give me one reason."

"No, just take it from me, I cannot spend the night with Billy Wentworth."

"But it's all set."

"Then it will have to be unset. I will not stay with Billy Wentworth."

"Do it for me."

"No."

"For your dad."

"No!"

"Bingo," his mom said, abandoning her efforts at soft-sell, "you are so interested in yourself and your own problems that you never even notice anyone else. It's one of your worst faults. You go through life like you are the only person with any problems. All your life is a crisis. You never think of anyone but yourself."

"I do. I'm interested in people. I spend half the school day going to the pencil sharpener just to see what they're doing."

"I'm not talking about spying on people."

"Mom—"

"I'm talking about the fact that you have not even noticed your own father lately."

"What about Dad?"

"He's quiet. He's withdrawn. He hates his work. The one thing he's got to look forward to is homecoming."

"He doesn't hate his work—"

"Can you honestly imagine that it's fun to sell insurance for a living?"

"Just get me a baby-sitter."

"Who?"

"I don't know—somebody."

"Well, I promise you one thing—*you* are the one who is going to have to tell your father. You are going to be the one to say, 'Dad, you cannot go to homecoming because I won't stay at the Wentworths.' You just get up off that bed right now and call him up on the phone. I mean it."

She pulled Bingo up and into the hall. She dialed the phone and said, "Sam, your son has something to say to you."

Bingo took the phone. "Dad?"

"What is it, son? I'm in sort of a hurry."

"I just wanted to tell you not to worry about me for homecoming weekend. I'm staying with the Wentworths." He handed the phone to his mom.

"Thank you, thank you," she said. "You are the most wonderful son in the world. I will never forget this. I'll make it up to you. I promise. Bingo, you are—"

"Leave me alone," he said.

THE TEST

"Test?" Mr. Markham said. "What test? Was I going to give you a test?"

Bingo didn't remember the test either, but then the knowledge that he was going to have to spend the night with Billy Wentworth had forced everything else out of his mind.

He had spent the whole night going over it. Would he sleep in the bottom bunk or the top one? Would Billy scorn his Superman pajamas?

"Yes," Mamie Lou said, "you told us to study for a test and so we did. Where's the test?"

"Thanks a lot," Billy Wentworth grumbled. "Now he'll give us one. He'd forgotten all about it. If anybody flunks, it's your fault."

"Gang," said Mr. Mark. "Mamie Lou is right. I said we were going to have a test and rather than disappoint those who studied, we are going to have a test."

He got up from his desk.

"So we have a problem—no test. But there is a simple solution to the problem. Get out your paper."

The class groaned.

"No, wait, you haven't heard this. You're going to like this. Give me a chance. Paper ready, everyone?"

The papers were ready.

"All right, I am going to let you make up your own history test. Yes, you heard correctly. You will make up your own questions. You will answer your own questions. They may be true-false questions, fill-in-the-blanks, or essay-type questions. The details are up to you."

He sat down at his desk. "Oh, yes. Gang, each test must consist of at least ten questions. Good luck."

Bingo decided instantly on fill-in-the-

130

blanks. That would be easiest. He would just write ten sentences about the Constitution and then he would underline one word in each sentence as if that were the blank.

Everyone was writing. No one was having problems with either the questions or the answers.

As usual, Bingo was one of the first to finish. Out of habit he glanced at his pencil, but he found he had no desire to sharpen it.

He reached under his desk for his journal. He flipped it open. He had pages and pages of burning questions by now. He had not even known there were that many burning questions in the entire world.

Can I be ill?

Can the fact that I have to spend the night with Billy Wentworth bring on a genuine illness?

Will my mom believe it is a genuine illness or will she claim I am faking?

Would she realize the seriousness of my not wanting to go to the pencil sharpener?

Will I stop wanting to do other things?

Will I end up without even the desire for burning questions?

He did not get to finish, because Mr. Markham was asking for their attention.

"I see that some of you are through. Several of you have even attempted to hand in your papers."

He stood up and walked around to the front of his desk.

"Now, gang, here's part two of the test. I am going to ask you to grade the tests yourself. Put your hands down. Yes, you will grade your own test. No, I do not want you to exchange papers. I am putting you on your honor to grade your own paper. If you are capable of making up your own test, you are capable of grading it.

"When you are finished, you will hold up your graded paper so that I can record the grade. Please make your A's large enough for me to read.

"Now are there questions? Yes, George."

"Can we make up all our tests from now on?"

"We'll see."

All day long Bingo had a hard time concentrating. Every time Billy Wentworth shifted in his seat, Bingo steeled himself for something like, "I hear you're spending the night with me, Worm Brain."

"Yes, I hope you don't mind," he would answer.

"Well, I do mind, so what are you going to do about it," he would say.

Then he would say, "I—"

"Bingo."

"What? What?"

Bingo looked up. School was over. The classroom was empty except for Melissa and him.

Melissa said, "Hi."

"Hi."

"I've been worried about you all day."

"Have you?"

"Yes, you didn't go to the pencil sharpener even one time."

"I didn't really feel like it."

"Is it because of what I told you?"

"What?"

"About Mr. Mark?"

"No, no, it wasn't that."

"I was worried because—you know—like sometimes you tell somebody something that worries you and it makes you feel better but it makes them feel worse, and I was worried that that was what I did to you."

"No, you didn't make me feel worse. You make me feel better."

"Really? You mean that?"

"Yes."

"Anyway, I found out Dawn's last name."

"You did?"

"It's Monohan. I asked Mr. Mark and he told me."

"Oh."

"So now I don't know whether to call her up or not. I'm really worried about Mr. Mark. If I knew she was his girlfriend, I'd feel better, wouldn't you?"

"Maybe."

"Because if she's his girlfriend, she would be helping him through things, and if she's not his girlfriend, then she wouldn't."

"Yes."

"So what do you think? Should I call or not?"

"I think you should call."

"Really? You aren't just saying that because you know I want to call?"

"No."

"Thank you, Bingo. I'll let you know what I find out. Bye."

"Bye."

Bingo got up slowly. Now he knew he was sick. He didn't even enjoy mixed-sex conversations anymore. With his head hanging, he started for home.

JOURNAL II

"MR. MARK?"

"Yes, Bingo."

"What are we supposed to do when our journals are full?"

"Well, let's worry about that when they are full, all right?"

"Mine is."

Mr. Mark looked up in surprise. "Your journal is full, Bingo?"

"Yes."

"Did you use just one side of the paper?"

"Both sides."

"Both sides are full?"

"Yes, sir."

"Of writing?"

"Well, there are some illustrations."

"But the journal is full?"

"Yes, sir. It's been full for three days, but I didn't have anything to write, so I wasn't worried about it."

"Is anybody else's journal full?"

No hands went up.

"Is anybody else's journal halfway full?"

No hands.

"A quarter full?"

Melissa put up her hand. Bingo glanced at her with gratitude.

"Well, Bingo, I guess I'll stop by the store on the way home and get another volume for you. In the meantime, can you make do with a few sheets of loose paper?"

"I don't have anything to write, Mr. Mark. I'm not even sure I'm ever going to write again."

"Oh?"

"I just wanted to know what you wanted us to do when our notebooks were full."

It was Friday. That night he would be sleeping in one of Billy Wentworth's beds. Against his will, he began sketching the beds on the last page of his journal.

When he drew himself on the top bunk, the lead broke and shot, bullet-like, across the aisle.

He got up slowly and went to the pencil sharpener. It was the first time he had been to the pencil sharpener all week.

He was grinding away, worrying about the supper, the bunk beds. He had even started worrying about the poodle. At that moment Bingo's thoughts were interrupted by a distinctive sound.

Bingo would have known that sound anywhere—the breaking of pencil lead. Bingo knew the pencil lead was Melissa's. He ground slower.

He watched the floor. Reeboks with plaid shoelaces came into view. It was Melissa. He looked up.

"It's a bad day for pencils." She grinned and showed him the broken lead.

He said, "Obviously."

He took out his pencil and blew off the shavings. He wished he had blown them in the opposite direction. However, Melissa didn't seem upset that they landed on her. Bingo liked women who were not easily offended.

To give Melissa the opportunity to brush them off, he said, "I better empty this."

He untwisted the pencil sharpener and went to the trash can. Mr. Markham said, "What are you doing, Bingo?"

"Emptying the pencil sharpener."

"There's nothing in it."

"Oh. So there isn't."

Bingo went back to the pencil sharpener. Melissa had been waiting for him. She whispered, "I tried to call—" She glanced at Mr. Markham. "—you know who."

"Who?"

"You know."

With the eraser of her pencil, she wrote D A W N on the windowsill. Bingo said, "Oh."

"But guess what?"

"What?"

"She's got an unlisted number."

Mr. Markham said, "What's going on over there?"

"I was just going to my seat."

"That sounds like the first good idea you've had all day, Bingo."

Bingo said, "Excuse me," to Melissa

139

and started to squeeze past her. At that moment, something unexpected happened—something Bingo couldn't have planned in a million years.

Harriet jumped up to sharpen her pencil and for a moment Bingo was sandwiched between them like the filling in an Oreo cookie.

Harriet said, "Bingo!" in a disgusted way, as if he had done it on purpose.

Bingo said, "Sorry."

"Well, watch it."

"I will from now on."

"Bingo," Mr. Markham said tiredly.

"These things happen," Bingo explained. Then he went directly to his seat.

Well, now he had the answer to at least one of his questions. One mystery was solved.

He had been embraced by both girls at the same time, and when he drew the picture, he decorated Melissa with plus marks and Harriet with minuses.

When he got his new journal and if he survived the weekend, he would start a new section—*Questions that Burn No More.*

If—he repeated for emphasis—he survived the weekend.

DOUBLE-DECKER MISERY

BINGO LAY in the top bunk bed. He had been there for ten minutes and he was miserable. He had to go to the bathroom.

He told himself that he could not possibly have to go again, that he had gone five times since supper. He reminded himself that he did not want to climb down from the top bunk, that there was no ladder.

The bunk-bed set was modern Western, and in going over the wagon wheel at the foot of the bed, Bingo had hurt himself on one of the spokes.

He had not cried out in pain—he was grateful for that—but he knew that if it happened again—and in the dark it was bound to—he would cry out.

It had been a very long evening. The only relief had come after supper when Bingo pretended to have forgotten something.

"I'll be right back," he told the Wentworths.

"You want Billy to go with you?"

"No, it won't take me but a minute."

He went home, unlocked the door, and walked through the painfully empty rooms. He went in the bathroom to look at himself in the mirror.

The face looking back at him was pitiful. He must have looked this bad when his parents left him. How could they have left?

Bingo recalled the last moment in the front yard. He had stood with his knapsack hanging from one hand, the other hand lifted in a farewell gesture.

"See you Sunday," his mom called.

He nodded.

He hoped for one brief moment that they would turn and say, "Oh, it was just a joke, Bingo. You didn't really think we'd leave you. Oh, he really thought we were going."

"Bye!"

They got in the car and slammed the door. His mom was laughing. As they started down the street, she rolled down the window and blew the trumpet.

"Bingo?"

It was Billy Wentworth's voice. Bingo could not let Wentworth see him looking at himself in the mirror. Quickly he flushed the toilet and came out in the hall.

"My dad's taking me to the movies. *Rambo III*. Want to come?"

"Yes."

"It's better than *Rambo II*, but not as good as *Rambo*. Which one did you like best?" Billy asked as they crossed the lawn together.

"I liked them all the same." Bingo had never seen either, but he instinctively knew he had spoken the truth.

While Bingo was reliving the experience of *Rambo III*, much of which he had watched with his eyes shut, a miracle happened.

Bingo fell asleep.

It was Saturday. Bingo heard the familiar sounds of cartoons. In his eagerness to be in front of the TV, he almost threw his feet over the side of the bed and jumped off.

He opened his eyes and was instantly grateful he had not leapt. If he had, he would have fallen six feet to Billy Wentworth's floor and broken both his legs.

He spent a few moments looking at Billy Wentworth's ceiling. This was the closest he had ever been to a ceiling. Then he leaned over the side of the bunk.

The bottom bunk was empty. That was something else to be grateful for. He would not have to climb over the wagon wheel with Billy watching him.

Bingo climbed down from the top bunk carefully. He found his clothes. He put them on. He went into the living room. Billy's sister said, "Everybody's in the kitchen," without looking at him.

"Thank you."

Mrs. Wentworth said, "Good morning, Bingo. We just fix our own breakfasts around here. There's plenty of cereal. Help yourself."

"I will."

Mr. Wentworth was reading the paper, but he paused to say, "Midge tells me your parents went to Catawba College."

"Yes, sir, they've gone back for homecoming."

"Is that a Baptist college?"

"No sir, they both majored in marketing."

Billy said, "Mr. Markham says there's no point in going to college."

"Oh, I'm sure Mr. Markham didn't say that," Mrs. Wentworth said mildly.

"Yes, he did, didn't he, Bingo?"

"Maybe. I've missed a few things this past week."

"He also said that by the time we got

145

out of kindergarten we'd learned all we needed to know—to share, not to hit people, to say we're sorry when we hurt somebody, and to hold hands when we go out in the world."

Mr. Wentworth said, "That doesn't mean there's no point in going to college."

"Well, he must not believe in going to college. He's stopped teaching us, hasn't he, Bingo? How are we going to get into college if he doesn't teach us anything?"

"I don't think he's stopped teaching us," Bingo said. "Maybe he's slowed down a little."

"Don't exaggerate, Billy."

"Mom, he doesn't teach us a thing. He really doesn't. We write in our journals, we make up our own tests, we even grade our own tests. Every single person gave themselves an A."

"Now, Billy—"

"Mom, I'm not exaggerating. Am I, Bingo?"

"We did grade our own tests, Mrs.

Wentworth, and there were a lot of A's, but Mr. Markham does stuff like that to keep us interested."

"I don't think his elevator goes all the way to the top floor," Billy said.

"How many times have you made your own tests?"

"Just once, but, Mom—"

Something cold touched Bingo's ankle, and he quickly crossed his legs. It was the poodle again.

The poodle had an unsettling way of sniffing a certain spot on Bingo's leg. Bingo couldn't stand it—the touch of that little tiny cold nose, the brush of those whiskers . . .

Bingo was going home this morning and spraying his legs with insect repellent.

While he was there, he would call Melissa. At last he had a good reason to do that—to let her know that he was at Billy Wentworth's. "I was afraid you might have tried to call me—to tell me something about Dawn—and you would worry when you didn't get an answer," he would say.

As it turned out, he didn't even need a reason. She said, "Oh, I'm so glad to hear your voice, Bingo."

"You are? I called because I was afraid you might have tried to call me—"

"I did. I called and called. I saw her."

"You saw Dawn."

"Yes. At Pizza Inn. She was having a small pepperoni with double cheese. She and a girlfriend were sharing."

"Oh."

"I went over and she didn't know me at first. I had on a headband so I said that I was Melissa and I was in Mr. Markham's room. I said, 'Remember I talked to you when he went in the Winn Dixie for hotdogs?'"

"What did she say?"

"She said, 'Oh, him,' like that. I said, 'Aren't you his girlfriend anymore?' She had told me she wasn't, but I pretended I had forgotten. She said, 'I never was his girlfriend. Never! He might say I was his girlfriend, but I wasn't and I never will be.' I said, 'Do you ever see him anymore?' She said, 'Not if I can help it. I hear his motorcycle and I hide. I get down behind the sofa. He scares me.' I didn't know what to say so finally I said, 'Did you get our letters? Our whole class wrote you letters.' "

"Maybe she wouldn't take them."

"She said, 'Oh, those letters. They really upset me. Imagine him talking about me in front of the class. What did he tell you? Did he say he couldn't go on living without me? Because I hate him saying that.' "

Bingo loved it when she did Dawn's voice. Even though he had never heard Dawn, he knew exactly how she sounded.

"I must have looked hurt because, Bingo, I worked hard on my letter, didn't you?"

"Yes."

"So she saw that and said, 'Oh, they

were wonderful letters.' She jumped up and hugged me. 'I loved the letters, but I'm the kind of person that if I don't like somebody, then I just plain don't like them and all the letters in the world won't change my mind. If I got a letter from the President of the United States, it wouldn't change one thing. Plus I'm dating a guy named Randy now.' "

Bingo waited.

"Then I didn't know what to say, would you have?"

"No."

"Bingo, I always feel so much better when I talk to you. You always say just the right thing."

"Oh, well . . ."

"So then we heard a motorcycle turning into the parking lot. Dawn thought it was Mr. Mark and said, 'Oh, where can I hide? Should I get under the table or have I got time to make it to the restroom?' "

Bingo settled back in his chair for a long chat.

"And I said, 'That's not Mr. Mark's bike. His is . . .' "

THE LETTERS

BINGO OPENED his new journal and smoothed the first page. He wrote, *This book is dedicated to the new, improved Bingo Brown.*

Ever since his parents had returned home safely, he had felt like a new person. He even acted that way. He had not made any mention of his own weekend discomforts. He had been genuinely interested in what they had done.

"Oh, Bingo," his mom had said, "it was so much fun. I laughed so hard I almost couldn't play the trumpet."

"That's good. How was your handstand, Dad?"

"We didn't do the handstands. We did a pyramid. They were a little wobbly."

"A little wobbly! They were hilarious. I laughed till I cried."

"They weren't that funny."

"You didn't see them from the rear." She laughed and turned to Bingo. "Oh, Bingo, I hope you're going to go to Catawba. It's so much fun."

"I do want to learn something," Bingo answered.

"But having a good time is important too. College is the last free time in your life. I want you to promise me something, Bingo."

"What?"

"I want you to promise that when you go to college, you're not going to be one of those boys who spends his life in the library and jumps like a scared rabbit every time a girl looks at him."

Bingo was too stunned to speak. *He* jump when a girl spoke to him! He, who had been in love three times in one day and had already had four mixed-sex conversations!

"Get out paper and pencils, gang," Mr. Markham said. "I want you to do something special today."

"I thought we were going to write in our journals," Bingo said.

Mr. Markham shook his head. "I've got something I really need for you to do."

Billy Wentworth turned and gave Bingo a knowing look.

"Now, gang, this is really important. I'm going to have you write letters, and this is probably the most challenging assignment I'll ever give you."

Bingo closed his journal reluctantly.

"Now does everybody have paper? Pencils? Nobody needs to sharpen?"

He glanced at Bingo. Bingo shook his head.

"Good."

Mr. Markham moved around his desk and stood with his hand on the imaginary beard. He looked up at them with eyes that were fever-bright.

"Suppose, gang," he said, "that one of your friends—and this doesn't have to be a friend your own age. It could be someone older, but it should be someone you admire, someone you care about. Let's say it could be someone in high school, maybe a Little League coach, but it's a friend you care about."

Mr. Markham paused thoughtfully. "Now you have come to suspect—no, let's make it stronger than that. You don't suspect, you *know* that this person is thinking about committing suicide. You don't want to tell anybody, because you don't have any proof. You could be wrong—you aren't sure, but your gut feeling tells you that this person is going to commit suicide. So you decide to write this friend a letter and talk him out of it. So this is the most important letter you will ever write because a life depends on your words."

Mr. Markham leaned back on the desk and looked at them. "Have you got any questions before you get started? Yes, Mamie Lou?"

"Are we supposed to use the name of

a real person or do we make up some-body?"

"I don't want a real name. Let's see. How about *Dear Friend?*"

He looked around the room. "No more questions? All right, then, get started." Mr. Markham walked around his desk. Before he sat down he said, "I'm going to give you as much time as you need on this, gang. I want these letters to be as good as you can make them."

Bingo had been prepared to write in his journal and he couldn't get his mind on his letter. He wrote *Dear friend,* and then he looked around the room.

Nobody else was doing any better than he was. Not one single person was writing.

Finally Harriet raised her hand.

"Yes, Harriet?"

"I'm not having much luck."

"How do you mean?"

"I can't get started."

There were a few mutters of, "Me either."

Mr. Markham got up. "How many are in trouble?"

Every hand went up.

"All right, let's talk about this for a little bit. *Dear Friend.* You've gotten that far, I assume. *I know that you are thinking about suicide.*"

There was a flurry of activity as everyone copied the first line. Then they looked up.

Mr. Markham sighed. "Gang, this is not a lesson in dictation. All right, I'll give you one more line and then you're on your own. I don't care how many pitiful looks you give me." He glanced up at the ceiling. *"Dear friend, I know that you have been thinking of suicide. Please do not take your life because—"* He stopped.

He said, "Now, that's all the help I'm going to give you. These are your letters. It's your friend in trouble. Maybe," he went on more slowly, "it's the word *friend* that's bothering you. Maybe it's not specific enough. Suppose it's the boy down the street who plays catch with you every afternoon after school. So you think selfishly at first. You don't want this boy to kill himself because then you won't have anybody to play catch with. Put that down. It's all right to be selfish. But then you start thinking."

Mr. Markham moved around to the front of his desk.

"You start thinking. The boy down the street who plays catch with you— and you probably aren't that much fun to play catch with—so this boy down the street is being nice, generous—what else? Kind, giving . . . So if this boy commits suicide then not only does he go out of the world but so does his kindness and goodness and generosity. And gang, the world can't afford to lose any more of that stuff. There's not enough of it as it is."

He stepped away from his desk, closer to the class.

"And gang, it's not the mean, rotten gangsters that commit suicide—well, okay, they do it but like Hitler did, to keep from being captured. I'm not talking about that. I'm talking about people that never hurt anybody in their lives. I'm talking about poets and short-order cooks and soft-spoken uncles and janitors. I'm talking about teachers."

He paused. He rubbed his hands together as if he were soaping them.

"Why wouldn't you want *me* to commit suicide? Think selfishly. Because you'd get a substitute teacher. Take it from there. Why wouldn't you want Aunt Gertie to commit suicide? Because every Christmas she sends you a twenty-dollar bill. Take it from there."

He looked at them for a long time. It was Mamie Lou who picked up her pencil first and began to write. Then Harriet. Then Bingo.

With a sigh Mr. Markham went back to his chair and sat down.

THE ALL-NEW IMPROVED BINGO

THERE WAS a note on Bingo's desk. He stood for a moment staring at it. He had never gotten a note before. He picked it up and turned it over, looking at it as if he didn't know what to do with it.

His name was on the front and there was a heart where the postage stamp would have been. In the heart was a face that looked like Melissa.

At that moment, Billy Wentworth turned around in his seat. "What was going on yesterday?"

"Yesterday?"

"Yeah, with you and Harriet."

"Oh, that." The incident with Harriet had been a disturbing one. Bingo had been going home when all of a sudden he heard someone say, "Bingo."

He glanced around so fast his neck popped.

"Over here."

"Harriet, what are you doing behind the tree?"

"I don't want him to see me."

"Him?"

"Billy! So would you do me a favor?"

"If I can . . ."

"Would you pretend to be talking to me?"

"I am talking to you."

"I mean, if I come out from behind the tree, would you talk to me."

Bingo was getting uneasy. "I guess so."

She stepped out. "And walk with me! Come on! Walk!"

Bingo walked, but it felt like a forced march. He didn't like it.

"Say something!"

"What?"

"Anything!"

Forced walking and now forced talking. How had he ever thought he loved this woman? Even if she did dedicate a concert to him, he wouldn't listen. He would put his fingers in his ears.

"Say something!"

"What?"

"Bingo—" She was speaking through her teeth now. "Billy saw me hide behind that tree so he probably thinks I was hiding there to watch his house. He's looking out the window right now. If he sees me with you, he'll think I was there to meet you. So say something!"

At last Bingo had something to say.

"This is my house, Harriet. Goodbye."

That was the whole unfortunate incident, and now Billy Wentworth wanted to hear about it. Bingo glanced across the room. Harriet was watching them with slitted eyes.

Billy said again, "What were you and Harriet doing in front of my house, Worm Brain?"

Bingo said, "Nothing. We weren't doing anything. We just walked past."

"It didn't look like you were just

161

walking past to me. It looked like she was hiding behind a tree and then you came along and she jumped out. I don't like people doing stuff like that in front of my house."

"Well, that is pretty much what happened," Bingo said. "I mean the part about her hiding behind the tree and jumping out at me." Bingo turned his head so that Harriet couldn't read his lips. "I think she likes you."

"Likes me?" Billy Wentworth said. It was so loud even Mr. Markham looked up. "She better not like me! I didn't tell her she could like me."

Harriet turned her head away and looked out the window. The back of her neck started getting red.

"Er, gang," said Mr. Markham, "may I remind you that you are supposed to be writing in your journals. If you have a message for a member of the class that cannot wait until recess, you may come up, give me the message, and I will relay it to the proper person." Mr. Markham said things like this a lot, but no one ever took him up on it.

This time Billy Wentworth got up out of his seat. He pulled down his Rambo t-shirt. He went to Mr. Markham's desk.

"I take it, Billy, you have a message for someone," he said.

"That's right."

Everyone in the class stopped writing.

Mr. Markham said, "So, who is the message for? Perhaps you could whisper it so as not to disturb the rest of the class."

Billy Wentworth was not a good whisperer. "Harriet!"

"Perhaps you might like to write the message down. Here's a notepad. The rest of you get back to work."

Billy's message appeared to be two words in length. When he finished writing he underlined the words twice and then went back to his desk.

Mr. Markham put his fingers up to his head as if he had a headache. He said, "If I judge that your message should not be passed on, then I will destroy it. If you see me destroy your message, that means I do not deem it worthy of being passed on."

Mr. Markham took the top sheet of the notepad and tore it into small pieces. Then he noticed that Billy had borne down so hard the message was on the next four sheets. He tore those up too.

In the silence that followed, Bingo opened his note. It said, "Meet me at the flagpole after school. M."

Bingo looked across the room. He nodded.

Mr. Markham said, "Bingo, is there something wrong with your neck?"

"No."

"Then why are you nodding like one of those dogs on car dashboards?"

"I was nodding because I thought something was wrong with my neck. Then after I nodded, I discovered nothing was wrong with my neck."

"That's the first good news I've had all week."

When the bell rang, Bingo was out of his seat like a shot. He had to avoid Harriet and Billy Wentworth and get to the flagpole. He was waiting there when Melissa came down the steps.

"Oh, you went out of the room so fast, I thought you weren't going to wait."

"No, I wanted to wait." Bingo put his hands over his back pocket where the note was.

"Well, it wasn't really important— just that I found out where Dawn works."

"You did?"

"In the Nautilus. That health club. She teaches aerobics."

"I didn't know that."

"My sister's boyfriend is a member there."

"I didn't know that either."

Bingo couldn't really enjoy this mixed-sex conversation because he had to watch out for Harriet and Billy Wentworth.

There she was, coming down the steps, heading right for him. Her face was purple.

Bingo said, "I've got to go. I'll call you later."

As he ran down the street, he was amazed at how casual he had become, at how easily he had come up with that. *I'll call you later.*

Am I a man at last?

He glanced over his shoulder. Harriet was gaining on him. He ducked his head and ran for his life.

CALLS FOR BINGO

THE PHONE rang.

"I'll get that," Bingo called cheerfully. "Hell-o!"

He had started singing out the word. He loved the telephone. In some ways mixed-sex conversations were better by

166

phone. You didn't have to worry about your expressions.

A voice said, "It's me—Harriet."

Bingo fumbled the phone as if it had suddenly gotten too hot to handle.

"Oh?"

"I want you to do something for me."

"I'm not very good at doing things for people," he reminded her.

"You're the only person that can do this."

"What is it?"

"Go over to Billy Wentworth's and tell him I don't like him."

"I can't do that. I—"

"You've got to!"

"Why me?"

"Because you're the one that told him I did like him." She lowered her voice but unfortunately he could still hear her. "See, Bingo, I really do like him and the only way I can get him to like me is to make him think I don't like him."

"Harriet, I'm sorry. My mom's calling me to supper."

"It's only four o'clock."

"We eat early."

Bingo hung up the phone and went into the living room. "If I get any more phone calls, I'm not here."

His mom said, "Oh?"

"If I tried to tell you what had happened to my life, you would say it was my fault."

"No, I wouldn't."

"Yes, you say I create crisis, and, Mom, I don't create crisis, but I'm always standing right next to it. It's like I'm living my life in the middle of all these little tornadoes and I get swept into them and it's not my fault. I'm helpless."

"What's happened now?"

"Yesterday this girl—Harriet—was spying on the Wentworths' house and I was passing by—totally innocent—and Harriet leaped out and demanded that I talk to her, and I said a few words, and then she demanded that I walk with her, and I took four steps, five at the most. This morning Wentworth asked me about it and I thought he thought this girl and I were—" He broke off. "Oh, it's too complicated. Just go ahead and say, 'Bingo, it's your fault.' It will save a lot of trouble."

The phone rang then and Bingo pulled a sofa pillow in front of his heart for protection. "Remember, I'm not here," he said.

Bingo lay in bed in his Superman pajamas. His mom knocked at the door. "Bingo, are you asleep?"

"Of course not."

"The phone's for you."

"I told you I wasn't here."

"She said to tell you it was about Mr. Mark and it was real important."

Bingo threw back his Superman cape. "Did she tell you her name?"

"Melissa."

"Oh, that's different." Bingo was at the phone in two strides. "Hell-o."

"I know it's too late to be calling," Melissa said, "but I had to tell you about something awful that happened at the Nautilus."

"The Nautilus?"

"Where Dawn works. Remember I told you that my sister's boyfriend goes there?"

"Yes."

"So anyway, late this afternoon Mr. Mark came to the Nautilus. He wasn't supposed to come anymore, because Dawn doesn't want to have anything to do with him. Anyway, he tried to make her get on the motorcycle and the man—Stevie—who's the manager came out and he and Mr. Mark had a fight—well, it wasn't really a fight because Stevie is into body-building and Mr. Mark hardly has any muscles at all. Stevie punched him out—that's what my sister's boyfriend said, and Mr. Mark rode off so fast he almost hit a lady with a grocery cart."

Bingo didn't say anything.

"I just feel so sorry for Mr. Mark, don't you?"

"Yes."

"You aren't mad that I called you, are you?"

"No, I'm not mad."

"Oh, good, I couldn't stand it if you were mad at me, Bingo."

Bingo hung up the phone and stood for a moment in his sagging Superman pajamas. His mom was watching him from the doorway. "Another tornado?" she asked.

He nodded. He pulled his Superman cape around him as if he were shielding himself from the world.

"Good night," he said.

BOEHMER!

BINGO CAME up the school steps slowly. He was deliberately late because there were so many people he did not want to see—Harriet, Billy Wentworth, the punched-out Mr. Markham. He didn't even want to see Melissa. Lately Melissa seemed to think he wanted to know more than he really did about things.

171

He stepped inside the front doors. He had thought the hall would be deserted, that he would walk unobserved to class, taking his time, preparing himself to open the door. But his entire class was in the hall, clustered at the door of the classroom.

Melissa ran toward him. "Bingo, Boehmer's in our room! Boehmer!"

"What's he doing in there?"

"Nobody knows."

"Is Mr. Mark there?"

"No, just Boehmer. Everybody thinks we must have done something!"

"What?"

"That's just it. We don't know. But if one of us had done something, we'd be called to his office, wouldn't we, so it must have been all of us."

Bingo and Melissa walked slowly to the classroom door. They joined the back of the group. There was an air of apprehension. The whispered questions, the lack of answers—Bingo could not remember a moment so filled with dread.

He peered around heads. Boehmer was there all right, reading some papers on Mr. Markham's desk. It looked like it might be their letters.

The late-bell rang, causing the apprehension to grow.

"Should we go in or what?" Mamie Lou asked.

Tara said, "We have to go in, don't we?"

"Yes," said Harriet, "we can't be late in front of Boehmer."

"Then go in," someone said from the safety of the back of the crowd.

There was a push, and three students—Harriet, Tara, and George Roges—popped unwillingly into the room. The rest followed, and silently they went to their seats.

Bingo's heart had started pounding. He positioned himself directly behind Billy Wentworth, grateful for once for Billy's size. Bingo did not want to be noticed.

Mr. Boehmer was still engrossed in

the papers. Finally he looked up and took off his glasses.

"Boys and girls," he said, "I've had some very bad news this morning about Mr. Markham. He was in a motorcycle accident last night. We just found out about it."

Everyone inhaled the news. It was an audible sound, and then there was silence.

The furnace had been turned on for the first time that morning, and the only sounds in the room were the crack of unused pipes, the faint hiss of steam.

Despite the heat from the radiators, Bingo was cold. The chill started in his feet, moved up his legs, and now flooded his stomach.

He had expected the worst, but he had thought the worst would be that he himself was in trouble. Under his desk, his knees began to tremble. He pressed them together.

He knew accidents happened. He had read about them in the newspaper and seen them on TV. But up until this moment, the only accidents he had really worried about were those that could happen to him.

Bingo's reaction was all physical. First the coldness, then the trembling, and now his throat began to tighten. He felt as if he had been the victim of an accident himself.

"Yes, Melissa?"

"I don't believe it."

Even in his state of shock, Bingo was aware that Melissa would be the one to speak for all of them.

"I'm afraid it's true. I felt the same way when I heard it. Yes, Mamie Lou?"

"Is he hurt bad?"

"He's in intensive care. He has some broken bones and a head injury. He was not, as I understand it, wearing his helmet."

"He always wore his helmet," Billy Wentworth said. "I never saw him without his helmet."

Bingo tried to say, "Me neither," but no sound came out.

"That may be, but it's my understanding that this time he was not wearing it. He was apparently traveling at a high rate of speed. He was alone. No other traffic appears to have been involved."

Mr. Boehmer glanced down at the papers on Mr. Markham's desk. Then he looked up and said, "Yes, Billy?"

"Where did it happen?"

"It was on Highway 64. He ran off the road on a curve and apparently struck a tree. The accident happened about eleven o'clock but he was not found for several hours. A passing motorist noticed his headlight in the weeds. Yes, Melissa?"

"Will he be all right?"

"I don't know. Even the doctors don't know at this point. He doesn't have any family in town, so I'm going over as soon as your substitute teacher arrives, to see if there's anything I can do. When I get back, I'll stop by and let you know what I've found out. Yes, Harriet?"

"If we wrote Mr. Mark some letters, could you take them to him?"

"I'd be glad to. That's a good idea. He may not be able to read them right away, but I know he would appreciate your writing them."

Bingo tore a sheet of paper from his new journal, the one dedicated to the new, improved Bingo. He got a pencil.

He wrote *Dear Mr. Mark*.

He looked around the room. Once again they were all in trouble together. Nobody was writing.

"Take your time," Mr. Boehmer said.

They bent over their papers. For once, Bingo didn't have to go to the pencil sharpener to see what they were writing. They all had the same sad message.

Please get well.

Miss Brownley was reading aloud. She had said, "I know you're too upset to concentrate—I am too. So why don't we just read this morning."

Bingo was slumped at his desk. He was not listening to the words. He had no idea what the story was about. Like everyone else, he was waiting for Mr. Boehmer. From time to time his knees trembled, like the aftershock of an earthquake.

Halfway through chapter eleven, there were footsteps in the hall, a knock at the door.

"It's Boehmer," someone said.

"Come in," Miss Brownley called.

Mr. Boehmer opened the door. For the first time in Bingo's life, he was glad to see him. "Am I interrupting?" Mr. Boehmer asked.

"No, come in, come in. We've been waiting for you."

Mr. Boehmer stepped inside the room. "Well," he said, "I can't tell you much more than I told you this morning. Mr. Markham has not regained consciousness. He's still in intensive care. His condition is listed as critical. I spoke to one of the doctors and he said all they can do right now is wait."

There was a pause. Tara put up her hand. "Did you see him?"

"Just for a minute."

"Can we see him?"

"No, he's not allowed any visitors. Maybe at a later time. I'll let you know."

"I want to take up a collection and send flowers," Melissa said.

"I'd hold off on that, Melissa, until he can appreciate them. I did leave your letters with the nurse, and she'll see that he gets them as soon as he feels like reading."

Mr. Boehmer looked around the room. "Any other questions?"

Bingo shook his head in silent dismay. He who had had hundreds of questions in his life, now found that at this crucial moment, he didn't have a one.

He leaned forward and dropped his head into his hands.

ROUTE 64

"MR. MARKHAM?" Bingo's mom asked. She sat down as hard as if she'd been pushed. "Not Mr. Markham."

Bingo nodded.

"I can't believe it. Mr. Markham?"

"Yes."

"Is he going to be all right?"

"I've told you all I know."

"Oh, not Mr. Markham. I hate that. How can we find out how—" Her head snapped up. "I heard the paper a minute ago. Maybe there'll be something about the accident in it."

She got up and pushed open the front door.

The afternoon paper was there, and she sat on the steps and began to flip through the pages. Bingo stood stiffly behind her.

"Here it is." She folded the paper back so she could concentrate on the article. She read it aloud.

"LOCAL TEACHER IN MOTORCYCLE ACCI-
DENT

A twenty-four-year-old Marshville man, John P. Markham—

"I didn't know he was only twenty-four, did you, Bingo?" Bingo shook his head.

"A twenty-four-year-old Marshville man, John P. Markham of Monroe Street, was the victim of a motorcycle accident Sunday night, according to Marsh County Sheriff Dwane Johnson.

"Dwane Johnson was kicked out of Catawba College, Bingo, I learned that at homecoming. He set off some sort of explosion during a rock concert. Let's see. Where was I?"

"—according to Marsh County Sheriff Dwane Johnson.

Markham was traveling north on

State Road 64, when his motorcycle went off the road, jumped a ditch and struck a tree.

"That's a terrible road. I don't even drive on it anymore unless I have to.

"Johnson said Markham was not wearing a helmet at the time of the accident.

"I'm surprised at that.

"Markham, who is a sixth-grade teacher at Roosevelt Middle School, is listed in critical condition at General Hospital.

"That's all it says," his mom said. "It doesn't mention what his injuries are. It doesn't mention his family. It hardly says anything."

"Mom, he has a head injury and some broken bones. I told you that. He's unconscious. What more is there to know?"

Bingo held out his hand for the paper and read the article for himself. "I wish I could go to the hospital and see him."

"Well, you can't. When someone's in intensive care they can only have one visitor an hour and it's got to be family."

"Mr. Boehmer says he doesn't have any family here."

"Oh, I hate that. Well, Marshville's not very far." She got to her feet abruptly. "Listen, I know Millie Hines who works in admittance. I'll give her a call. She might be able to find out some details."

She went inside and Bingo continued to stand on the steps, holding the newspaper. He couldn't remember feeling worse than this. It was as if Mr. Markham had taken Bingo off the road with him. Some of his body had gotten back to normal—his legs and stomach, but he still had to pull on his throat every time he wanted to swallow.

"Hey, Bingo!"

Bingo looked up. Billy Wentworth was at the edge of the drive on his bicycle. Bingo waved one hand without enthusiasm.

"You want to go see where it happened?" Billy shouted.

"What?"

"I found out where the accident happened, and I'm going to ride out there and see it. You want to come?"

"Yes." Bingo got his bike from the garage. He paused briefly to yell, "Mom, I'll be back later," and joined Billy Wentworth.

"It happened about three miles past the bowling alley, right side of the road," Billy said. "Let's go."

It had been a warm October, more like an extension of summer than fall, and today was the first cold day of the season. The leaves had already turned golden and red, but they had stayed on the trees, stubbornly refusing to fall.

Now as Bingo and Billy pedaled down the street, the trees relaxed their hold and the leaves began to rain down. In a

184

shower of gold and red, the boys headed for State Route 64.

They rode fast, leaning over their handlebars, pedaling hard until they were past the bowling alley, then they slowed down and coasted along the straight stretch before the curve.

Billy gave a signal and pulled off the road. "It must have happened here."

He leaned his bike against a tree and began walking back and forth, looking for clues in the deep weeds. Bingo stopped his bike, but he did not get off.

"It couldn't be here."

"Why not?" Billy called.

"Boehmer said on a curve."

"This is a curve."

"But I thought he meant that Mr. Mark didn't make the curve, like he was going too fast."

"That's what I thought too. But my mom talked to the ambulance driver and he said Mr. Mark went straight off the road. Look!" Billy Wentworth jumped the ditch.

"Look at what?" Bingo pulled his throat so he could swallow.

"The tracks. See, he hit right here. There's his tire mark."

"But if he went straight off the road, that would mean—" Bingo broke off. His fingers curled around his neck.

"Yeah, that would mean he did it deliberately." Billy Wentworth kept striding back and forth in the weeds. "This is the tree he hit. Look at the marks."

He pulled aside some leaves so Bingo could see the ruined bark.

"And look how all the weeds are trampled over here. This is it, I tell you! The ambulance pulled off right here. Mr. Mark landed right about—" he measured off a few steps "—here."

Billy stood in the center of the weeds with his arms outstretched.

Bingo stayed on the other side of the ditch. He held his throat with one hand, his handlebars with the other.

"Come see for yourself, if you don't believe me."

"I believe you."

Billy bent forward. "Here's something that looks like—" Suddenly Billy fell silent. He held onto a tree for support.

He swallowed. "This is it all right."

He walked toward Bingo slowly, touching trees as he came. He stepped over the ditch and went down on one knee.

"But why would he do that?" Bingo asked. "Why would he do it on purpose?"

Billy got up slowly. "Maybe there was a car. Boehmer wasn't here. He doesn't know everything. I got to rest a minute."

"You?"

Billy nodded. He leaned on the seat of his bicycle. "This was not the best idea I ever had," he admitted.

Bingo looked at Billy's pale face. For the first time Bingo felt like the stronger one.

"Are you all right, Billy?"

"Yeah, but I'm sorry we came."

"I am too."

"Don't tell anybody, but I can't stand the sight of blood. Even if I'm not sure it really was blood, it gets to me."

They rested on their bikes. The strength that had sent them speeding out here in a blaze of falling leaves was gone.

Finally Billy said, "I'm ready if you are."

Bingo nodded.

They turned their bikes around and slowly started for home.

NEWS AND MORE NEWS

BINGO CAME in the house slowly. He felt as if eight years had passed since he heard about the accident instead of eight hours. At any rate, he felt eight years older.

"Is that you, Bingo?" his mom called from the kitchen.

"Yes."

"Well, come on back. I've got some news."

Bingo went into the kitchen and leaned tiredly against the door.

"I called Millie, and she says Mr. Markham has regained consciousness. He's not out of the woods yet by any means, and there's no telling when he'll be out of the hospital, but he *is* conscious."

Bingo nodded.

His mother eyed him curiously. "I thought you would be so excited."

"I'm too tired to be excited. I just hate the whole thing."

"Well, of course, I do too."

"Not like me."

Bingo turned away. He took two steps into the dining room and then came back and leaned on the door again.

"I went out there and saw it."

"What?"

"The place where the accident happened."

"Bingo, I wish you hadn't done that."

"I do too."

She kept watching him. "That surprises me. It's not like you."

"I thought it might help me understand."

"Understand what?"

"How it happened . . . why it happened. I didn't even know it was going to happen."

"Of course you didn't know it was going to happen. No one can predict accidents."

Bingo looked down at his feet. For the first time he knew what his mother meant when she said, *You are so interested in yourself and your own problems that you never notice anyone else.*

"People have accidents all the time, Bingo," his mom went on. "People are careless. Remember my wreck? A woman in Head Hunters had given me a terrible body wave, and I glanced at myself in the rearview mirror and backed straight into a telephone pole.

190

Little things cause accidents most of the time."

"But not always."

"Bingo, you're making too much of this. Mr. Markham was on his way home. He was tired. He went off the road."

Bingo pulled at his throat. "It looked like he did it on purpose."

"No, Bingo, no. Now, I've met Mr. Markham. He isn't the type. There's an explanation. A dog darted into the road. He swerved to avoid a car. Any number of things could have happened."

"Mom," Bingo interrupted. "One time—this was last week—Mr. Mark had us write letters. And these letters were to someone who was thinking of suicide, to talk them out of it. Mr. Mark said these were the most important letters we would ever write in our lives. He said a person's life depended on them. And Mom, what worries me, what I can't get out of my mind—" He pulled at his throat, but this time it didn't let him swallow. "—what I keep thinking about and thinking about is that maybe we were writing the letters to him."

"Oh, no, Bingo, surely not."

"Yes, Mom, and maybe our letters weren't good enough. I mean, I didn't really try, because I thought it was stupid. But if I had known I was writing to him—that it was for real—if I had known that, then I really would have tried. I mean, maybe he went off the road because all of us thought the letters were stupid and didn't try."

He and his mother stared at each other across the kitchen. Then his mother came and put her arms around him. "Honey, your letters didn't have anything to do with it."

"How do you know?"

The phone rang and his mother tightened her grip on him. "Bingo—"

He turned his head toward the phone, and she put her hands on his face and turned him back. "Listen to me, Bingo."

"I better answer the phone."

"Let the phone go. I want to talk to you."

Bingo pulled away. "It might be for me. It might be about Mr. Mark."

His mother followed him to the phone, anxiously wiping her dry hands on her jeans.

He picked up the phone. "Hello."

"Bingo, is this you?"

"Yes."

"Well, it's me—Melissa."

Bingo looked up and met his mother's worried eyes. He said, "It's for me. You can go back to the kitchen. I'm fine."

His mom said, "I'll wait."

Melissa said, "I tried to call Dawn."

"You did?"

"Yes, I called the Nautilus and a man named Mike answered and said she wasn't there. I said I wanted to know if Dawn had heard about Mr. Markham's accident. Mike said, 'Is Mr. Markham the guy on the motorcycle?' I said, 'Yes, he's my teacher. Did she

193

hear?' Mike said, 'She heard. That's why she didn't come in today.' I said, 'Could you please give me her home phone number?' Mike said, 'No, she doesn't want anybody calling her.' I said, 'I hate to beg, but I have to talk to her.' He said, 'Well, give me your name and I'll have her call you.' So I gave it to him, but she hasn't called."

"Oh."

"I've been sitting by the phone for two hours. She should have called by now, don't you think? Or do you think it was just something Mike said to get rid of me?"

"I don't know."

"Because I've got to know what happened. I've just got to. I'm the kind of person who wants to know everything, Bingo. I've always been that way."

"Well, I did hear he's conscious. Someone at the hospital told my mom."

"I heard that too. But you know what really worries me? What really worries me is him not having on his helmet, doesn't it you?"

Bingo said stiffly, "Yes."

There was a pause and then Melissa said, "Bingo, you don't sound like yourself. Is there somebody there with you?"

"Yes."

"Is it your mom?"

"Yes."

"I knew it. Listen, you want me to call you back?"

"No, I'll see you at school tomorrow."

"All right, but come early so we can talk. I better get off the phone too and give Dawn a chance to call. Bye, Bingo."

Bingo hung up the phone. At once his mother said, "Now, listen to me, Bingo."

"I'm listening."

"Well, look at me."

Bingo looked up.

"I don't know whether your teacher went off the road on purpose or not. Maybe he did. But it was not up to you kids and your letters to stop him."

"But, Mom, if our letters had been really good—"

"No! Mr. Markham was your teacher, Bingo, and you looked up to him and trusted him and that was exactly what you should have done. Your teacher betrayed you."

"Mom, don't say that. He didn't betray us."

"Oh, yes, he did. A person is given a wonderful gift, Bingo—life. Life! And if he throws it away—as your teacher may have tried to do—if he throws it away, he's never going to get it back. Never! You can't change your mind next month and say, *Well, I'm tired of being dead. I think I'll pop back into the world.* It doesn't work that way. You slam the door shut, and you're never going to open it up again. To me, slamming that door is betrayal to everybody you slammed the door on, and it is the cruelest betrayal in the world."

Bingo looked at his mother. "Oh, Mom," he said. "I wish you'd been there last week to write a letter."

AFTER LUNCH

MELISSA WAS taking up money for Mr. Mark's card. "Does anybody have the right change?" she asked. "The card was ninety-nine cents, remember, so everybody owes three cents. Does anybody have exactly three cents?"

Melissa had on her Care Bears shirt with baby-blue barrettes holding back her hair. She looked anxiously around the room.

Bingo put up his hand.

"Bingo, you have the right change?"

He nodded.

She came back to his desk, smiling. "Oh, Bingo, thanks. Now I have your three cents and my three cents so I can make change." She picked up Bingo's pennies and turned around. "I can make change now, everybody. I—"

She broke off with a gasp. Boehmer was in the doorway. He said, "Am I interrupting?"

Bingo moved behind his shield—Billy Wentworth. He was grateful for whatever protection he could get these days.

"No, Mr. Boehmer, come in," Miss Brownley said. "We were just taking up money for a card for Mr. Markham."

"I won't take but a minute," Mr. Boehmer said.

Melissa said, "Scoot over, Bingo. I'll sit with you."

"What?"

"Scoot over."

Bingo couldn't move. If he scooted over even an inch, he would be in Boehmer's line of vision, and he'd have to scoot over a lot more than that to make room for a whole girl.

Melissa sat down and shoved him over with her hip. He gasped.

"I hope it's not bad news about Mr. Mark, don't you?" she said calmly.

He couldn't speak. He concentrated on making his face appear normal. He knew his face looked odd, tortured even, because this was the first time he had ever sat beside a girl, and while he had intended to sit by girls at a later time—in front of a TV set or a movie screen—he had never planned to do it in front of Boehmer. Sweat formed on his upper lip.

"Class," Mr. Boehmer said, "some of your parents have been talking to me."

There was an audible intake of breath at this betrayal by their parents. Normally Bingo would have worried that his mother had been one of them, because she was not the type to say something like, "I don't want to give my name, Mr. Boehmer, but—" She would say, "This is Bingo Brown's mother, and Bingo tells me that—"

But he had too many other things to worry about now.

"It was probably my mom," Melissa said to him.

Sweat poured down Bingo's face. His cheeks burned.

"Your parents have the feeling that some of you—actually, many of you have questions about Mr. Markham's accident and how he's getting along.

"Now, I haven't been very good, I'm afraid, in supplying answers. So I've asked a friend of mine, a doctor, who's seen Mr. Markham daily, to come in and talk to you. His name is Howard Gaston—Dr. Gaston—and he agreed to come and talk to you after lunch. You can ask him anything you want, all right?"

"I have tons of questions, don't you?" Melissa said.

Bingo shrugged.

"Well," Mr. Boehmer said, "that's all, class. You get back to what you were doing."

Mr. Boehmer went out of the room.

"Here, I'll leave this for you to sign," Melissa said. She put the card in front of him and got up.

Bingo looked down at the card. It was a long one. On the front was a bunch of bananas, and each banana had a smiling or hopeful face drawn on it. At the top were the words, *The whole bunch hopes you're feeling better.* Inside was the rest of the message. *And you're back hanging around with us again soon.*

Bingo flattened the card. He was surprised he was still capable of carrying out simple tasks. He wrote his name under the freckled banana that didn't look as hopeful as the rest.

Bingo could not eat lunch. This was Wednesday—pizza day—and so everyone in the cafeteria except Bingo was eating happily.

Ever since Mr.Boehmer had come in and announced that after lunch they could ask answers, Bingo had been blank. It was as if he didn't know what questions were.

He, the master of the question, had gone dry. He was an empty well. He had known all week that he would never again open his journal and have his pencil race across the page, writing questions one after another, so fast sometimes it skipped a *the* or *an*.

But it was even worse than that. He couldn't think of one single question.

Not one. He would never use the question mark again.

The bell rang, interrupting his miserable thoughts. Bingo got up. He took his tray with the untouched pizza to the counter. Then he walked back to his room.

Dr. Gaston had arrived and was at the desk, talking to Miss Brownley. He looked too young to be a doctor.

"Class," Miss Brownley said when they were seated, "this is Dr. Gaston, who's going to talk to you. Dr. Gaston, I'll let you take over."

Dr. Gaston said, "Boys and girls, first let me tell the good news. Your teacher has had no brain damage whatsoever—and that is very unusual considering the speed at which he was traveling and the fact that he was not wearing a helmet.

"So. That's the good news. The bad news is that he has a separated shoulder, a broken collarbone, a crushed upper arm. The left leg is broken in several places, as is the right ankle.

There is a crack in the seventh verte-brae. All in all, your teacher is very lucky to be alive and he knows this. Questions?"

There was such a long pause that Bingo was afraid the whole class was in the same fix he was—no questions. The doctor was going to have to go back to the hospital and tell Mr. Markham, "They didn't have a single question." Mr. Markham would be disappointed in them.

Bingo tried harder than ever to ask something.

Miss Brownley said, "I know some of them do have questions, Dr. Gaston, but it's like when my mother was sick, I could never think of questions to ask the doctor until I got home, and then it was too late. Oh, there's a hand."

It was Melissa, of course.

The doctor said, "Yes?"

"Did you tell Mr. Mark you were coming here?"

"Yes, I did. I told him I was coming

to talk to you, that some of you had questions."

"Did you talk to Mr. Mark about the accident?"

"We've discussed the accident, yes."

"Did he say why it happened?" Melissa asked. "Did he tell you why he went off the road?"

Dr. Gaston shook his head.

"Mr. Markham does not remember the time directly preceding the accident. This is not unusual in accident cases. He remembers starting home on his motorcycle. He was upset. He had been in an argument. He remembers passing the bowling alley. The next thing he remembers is waking up in the hospital twenty-four hours later."

There was another long pause. Billy Wentworth put up his hand.

"Yes?"

Billy Wentworth said carefully, "Some people went out there and looked at the place where the accident happened. These people said it looked to them like Mr. Mark went off the road on purpose."

The doctor said, "That is a possibility. It's also possible that something distracted him. We have no way of knowing, and unless Mr. Markham himself remembers, we never will know."

Melissa's hand was in the air again.

"Yes?"

"What do you think?"

"You mean about whether the accident was deliberate or not?"

"Yes."

"I can't answer that because I don't know. I wasn't there." The doctor paused. "I can tell you that Mr. Markham is very glad to be alive. He is in quite a bit of discomfort, and he is going to have a long recovery, but he is very glad to be alive. There's no question about that."

Melissa's hand was still in the air. "Did he tell you that in his own words?"

"Yes. He has said it several times

and there is no doubt in my mind that he means it."

Suddenly Bingo felt the first sense of relief he had known in days. At the same time, he leaned out of the protection of Billy Wentworth's back. With the tentativeness of a child taking a first step, Bingo raised his hand.

"Yes?"

"Did he say for you to tell us anything? Did he send us a message?" Not just one question, two!

"Oh, yes, I'm glad you reminded me." Dr. Gaston felt his pockets until he heard the rustle of paper. He took out a sheet of paper and unfolded it.

He read:

"Gang. Assignment. Imagine that your favorite teacher is in the hospital. He is lucky to be alive and he knows it. You don't have to convince him of anything. Just write and let him know how you are.
                    "Mr. Mark"

THE LOTTERY AND THE PRIZE

MISS BROWNLEY stood in front of the room with a shoe box. In the box were thirty-three slips of paper with names on them. After Miss Brownley shook the box, she was going to draw out two names. Those two people would get to go with her to the hospital on Saturday to visit Mr. Mark.

There was an air of excitement and hope at every desk except Bingo's. Bingo knew his name would not be picked. He had never been chosen for anything in his life.

Miss Brownley put the top on the shoe box and shook it. She lifted the lid and, without looking, reached inside.

Bingo leaned around Billy Wentworth to watch the proceedings.

Miss Brownley pulled one slip out.

"The first name is—" She read it to herself and smiled.

"Melissa."

Over the groans of disappointment was Melissa's gasp of delight. "I didn't think I'd get picked. I really didn't," she said. "I just can't believe I got it." She collapsed in her seat with pleasure.

"Lucky!" Harriet said.

Miss Brownley shook the box again. Then she reached in and pulled out a second slip. "The second name is—" She unfolded it, turned it around, read it and smiled.

That smile told Bingo it wasn't his name. He got ready to groan with the rest of them.

"Bingo."

She said the word the way it's said at bingo parlors when someone's a winner. She sounded as if she was genuinely glad he was going.

He said, "Me?"

"Yes, Bingo, you and Melissa will be going with me on Saturday. I'll get in touch with your moms."

When the buzz of disappointment had died, Bingo glanced across the room at Melissa. She was looking at him, smiling so brightly it was dazzling.

Billy Wentworth turned around in his seat. "Come over Saturday when you get back and tell me about it."

"I will."

"Next week we'll draw two more names," Miss Brownley said, "and we'll keep on doing this until everybody has had a chance to go to the hospital to see Mr. Markham, or until Mr. Markham is well enough to come see you."

Bingo was sitting on the front steps, waiting, when Miss Brownley pulled into his driveway that Saturday in her Toyota. Melissa was beside her on the front seat.

"They're here, Mom," he called quickly. "I'm going. Bye."

Bingo ran across the lawn so he could get away before his mom came out—

that was why he was on the steps in the first place—but she was too fast for him. She passed him at the azalea bushes.

"This is a very nice thing for you to do," she told Miss Brownley. Bingo got in the back seat.

"Oh, I wanted to do it," Miss Brownley said. "This has been hard for the kids, and I think it will help them to have Bingo and Melissa tell about seeing Mr. Markham. I was glad they were chosen, because they are good communicators."

To hide his pleasure and embarrassment, Bingo glanced out the car window. He saw Billy Wentworth standing at his living room window. Bingo waved but Billy stepped quickly out of sight, the way he himself had done when he was—might as well be truthful—spying.

Miss Brownley started the car and Bingo's mother called, "Behave yourself, Bingo."

Bingo knew his mom was going to

say something like that. What did she think he was going to do—run up and down the hall, disturbing sick people? Turn over wheelchairs? Couldn't she just once—

Melissa turned around and smiled. "My mom said the same thing." She had on a blue dress Bingo had never seen before. There were ribbons in her hair. She smelled strongly of ginger-snaps.

Bingo leaned back. Ever since his name had been drawn in what he now thought of as The Lottery, he had felt like a VIP. He could not have felt more important if his prize had been a million dollars.

He had seen lottery winners on the evening news occasionally, saying stupidly that they were going to keep on with their same old jobs, same old lives. Bingo couldn't understand that. He would buy race cars and airplanes and dash around the world.

Well, now he had won The Lottery, and he was keeping on with his same old life—going to school, coming home. He was even beginning to make up a few questions.

Melissa said, "Oh, I forgot my flowers!" She turned around. "Bingo, I forgot my flowers!"

Miss Brownley said, "It doesn't matter."

"But they were beautiful. I made a hole in a paper doily and stuck them inside. It was just beautiful."

"Mr. Markham wants to see you, not some flowers. Here we are."

They drove into the hospital parking lot and got out of the car. In silence they went in the hospital and got in the elevator. Miss Brownley punched Four.

Melissa glanced at Bingo. "I'm nervous, are you?"

Bingo nodded.

"I hope he looks like himself, don't you? I came to see my great-grandmother one time and I didn't hardly know her. She had always been real fat and nobody had told me she had gotten thin and—"

"This is our floor," Miss Brownley said.

Melissa couldn't finish about her great-grandmother.

Miss Brownley smiled. "Don't worry. It's going to be fine."

Mr. Markham was lying in the first hospital bed in room 419. His shoulder was in a cast. The rest of his body was hidden under the covers.

Bingo and Melissa paused in the doorway. Bingo wasn't sure he was going to be able to go any further. Something in his own shoulder had started to feel funny.

"Gang! Welcome!"

Bingo had to go in then, because Melissa grabbed his hand and pulled him. They walked to the side of the bed and stood there, holding hands.

This was the first time Bingo had ever held hands with a girl, but it was not romantic. Melissa was holding too tight. It was more a mutual-strength kind of thing.

"Bingo, Melissa, how are you?" Mr.

Markham looked thinner, paler, but his voice was the same.

Melissa said, "We're fine, Mr. Mark. We want to know how *you* are."

"How do I look? No lying now. You know I value honesty."

"Well, Mr. Mark, you don't look so bad as I was afraid you would."

"That is a great comfort to me. So what's going on at school?"

There was a pause and Miss Brownley filled it. "The class is doing real well, Mr. Markham, you'd be proud of them. I'm a poor substitute for you, I'm afraid."

"No, you're a good substitute," Melissa said loyally, "but we want Mr. Mark back."

Bingo cleared his throat. He knew it was his turn. He blurted out, "The pencil sharpener's broken."

"Oh, too bad, Bingo. I know what a hardship that must be for you."

"Yes, I hardly know what anybody's doing these days."

"Bingo." Mr. Markham looked disappointed. "I was counting on you to fill me in."

"Well, I did have to walk over to the trash can on Wednesday when we were all writing why we wanted to go on a field trip to the newspaper. See, only twenty people out of the whole school got to go."

"So why did they want to go, Bingo?"

"Well, Billy Wentworth wanted to go so he could get out of cleaning his room. Mamie Lou wanted to go because she may be an editor, if she doesn't get to be President. Freddie wanted to go because—maybe I shouldn't tell you. I don't want to disillusion you about Freddie."

"You couldn't, Bingo, believe me," Mr. Markham said with a faint smile.

"Freddie wanted to go to the newspaper because he thought he would see Snoopy there posing for Charles Schultz."

Mr. Markham bit his bottom lip. "Don't make me laugh. Whatever you do, Bingo, don't amuse me."

"I wasn't trying to."

"There, that's better. And why did you want to go, Bingo?"

"I didn't. I wrote the truth. I wrote that I had something better to do— come here and see you."

"That's what I wrote," Melissa said, beaming at Bingo. "That's exactly what I wrote."

The nurse came in. "That's it. Sorry."

Melissa said, "We just got here."

"Next time you can stay longer."

"But next time it won't be us. It'll be two different people."

"I'm sorry. Five minutes was the agreement."

"I've got to tell him one more thing." Melissa leaned over the bed. "My dad got a job."

"Oh, I knew seeing you two would make me feel better. Tell the gang I'll see them soon."

"We will." Bingo and Melissa backed out into the hall, waved with their free hands and started for the elevator.

Bingo was a little worried about the fact that he and Melissa were still holding hands. And he had no idea how to stop holding a girl's hand. Were you allowed to just let go? Would he and Melissa still be holding hands when they got to the car? How could they get in the car holding hands, with her in the front seat and him in the back? Would they have to hold hands out the window? Would Billy Wentworth see their hands and—

"Excuse me," Melissa said. "My hand's getting sweaty."

"Oh." So that was how it worked. "Mine too."

They wiped their hands—Melissa on the skirt of her dress, Bingo on his pants—and stepped onto the elevator together.

As they rode to the lobby, Bingo had a mature feeling. At last he was asking questions that had answers. You stopped holding hands with a girl when your hands got sweaty. It was simple, really.

Maybe he could have a section in his journal. *Questions with Answers.* He stepped off the elevator with new purpose in his stride.

Bingo lay in his bed. He was surprised to find that he still had that VIP feeling. It was not just because he'd been chosen to go to the hospital and see Mr. Mark, it wasn't because he'd held Melissa's hand or seen Billy Wentworth's envious face peering out the window.

This feeling was because of the little parts of the past week, things he normally might not have noticed. Like Miss Brownley smiling when she read his name. Like her saying she was glad he was chosen because—how had she put it—because he was a good communicator. It was Mr. Markham seeming glad to see him. It was making Mr. Markham bite his bottom lip to keep from smiling.

A person who was still swirling

around in his own personalized tornado would have missed those little things.

"Misty!" Mrs. Wentworth called outside his window. In the living room his parents laughed at something on television.

But in Bingo's bedroom there was only a sigh of contentment as Bingo pulled his Superman cape closer around his shoulders and fell asleep.

The publishers hope that this
Large Print Book has brought
you pleasurable reading.
Each title is designed to make
the text as easy to see as possible.
G.K. Hall Large Print Books
are available from your library and
your local bookstore. Or, you can
receive information by mail on
upcoming and current Large Print Books
and order directly from the publishers.
Just send your name and address to:

G.K. Hall & Co.
70 Lincoln Street
Boston, Mass. 02111

or call, toll-free:

1-800-343-2806

A note on the text
Large print edition designed by
Kipling West.
Composed in 18 pt Plantin
on a Xyvision 300/Linotron 202N
by Stephen Traiger
of G.K. Hall & Co.